Deeply Rooted

Marc Worthy

Copyright © 2024

All Rights Reserved

ISBN: 978-1-963919-37-0

Dedication

I dedicate this book to my grandmother Ms. Helen Worthy (Missy Bird).

Acknowledgment

First, I give honor to God for giving me the strength and ability to win souls through my words.

Next, I praise my family for their never-ending support and encouragement. To my mother, Ms. Barbara Worthy, I send a special thank you for your love and upliftment.

Last but not least, to my friends and associates, I say thank you for your encouragement.

Table of Contents

DEDICATION IV
ACKNOWLEDGMENT VI
ABOUT THE AUTHOR XII
PREFACE XIV
CHAPTER 1 GIVING BACK TO GOD 1
    DEEPLY ROOTED 2
    FAITH 6
    MY SHADOW 8
    MISSING U 10
    WHEN I THINK OF HOME 12
    HAVING THE LIGHT 14
    LIFE OF SIN 17
    JESUS HELP 19
    ONE FLESH 22
    NO JUSTICE IN MAN 24
    SMILE 27
    TEMPTATION 30
    THE MAN THAT I CAN BE 32
    PILLAR IN THE CHURCH 34
    BRING ON THE FIRE 37
    WALK, STAND, SIT 41
CHAPTER 2 ALL ABOUT LOVE 44
    LOVE SPELL 45
    LOVE ONE ANOTHER 48
    DEFINING THE WORD LOVE 50
    IT COULD HAVE BEEN ME 52
    SILENT FRIEND 55
    TEDDY BEAR 56

Tickle Yo' Ribs	58
A Boring Day	60
The Package	62
A Rare Find	64
Gods Child	67
Time to Shine	69
CHAPTER 3 HURT	**71**
Wishing	72
So Cold	75
Dangerous Game	77
Hurt	79
Tell Me If U Care	82
Blessing Blocker	84
Paper-Thin	87
Crooked Cop	89
Walking in the Sand	91
In the Hood	93
Street Wars	95
When I Consider How My Life Is Spent	98
CHAPTER 4 TRIALS AND TRIBULATIONS	**100**
Locking Me Up	101
Future Star	103
Time	105
Please Go Away	107
In a Shell	109
Lost	111
Smoking Kills	114
With This Rock I Thee Wed	116
My Heart	119
Smelling Myself	122
Growing Up Fast	124

- FEELING FREE ... 127
- THE OLD ME ... 130
- PUT IT DOWN ... 132
- BRING BACK THE OLD SCHOOL ... 134
- ALL ABOUT MONEY ... 136
- LET IT RAIN ... 138
- SLEEP ... 140
- AFRICAN QUEEN ... 142

CHAPTER 5 FAMILY VALUES ... 144
- DOWN BUT NOT OUT ... 145
- THANKSGIVING ... 147
- MISSY BIRD ... 149
- BABY GIRL ... 151
- THE LOVE TO MOM ... 154

CHAPTER 6 ROOTS AND WAR ... 156
- BLACK MAN ... 157
- "WORDS" ... 161
- WE THE PEOPLE ... 163
- WISING UP ... 165
- AMERICA, PLEASE UNDERSTAND ... 167
- EYES ... 170
- COMING TOGETHER ... 172
- WE SPEAK ... 174
- CONFUSED ... 176
- RIGHT TO SPEAK ... 178
- WALKING A STRAIGHT PATH ... 180
- LANGSTON HUGHES ... 182
- M. L. KING ... 185
- ANOTHER SOLDIER LEAVES BEFORE HIS TIME (ODE TO TUPAC) ... 188
- SITTING BACK ... 193
- WHO SCORE ... 195

BEGINNING OF THE END 198
THE EXCELLENCY OF WISDOM 200

About the Author

Marc Worthy is a prolific spoken word artist known for his ability to express himself through poetry. He is a native of Winston-Salem, NC, where he was born and raised. Marc attended and graduated from East Forsyth High School, where his inspiration for spoken word began and his gift was recognized. He combined his love for God, youth, and community, and his poems began to flow. His declaration of words reflects his lived experiences.

Marc is a godly man who believes that if he touches one person through his works, he has done something great. He believes that within God's word lies the answer to dilemmas and within his words lies the hope of mankind.

Preface

A few years back, I moved to Winston-Salem, NC from my hometown of Greensboro, NC. Although my home was only twenty-five miles from where I resided, I felt very homesick. One of the first people I met upon my arrival was Marc Worthy. He embodied all of what I learned was beautiful about the town itself. The warm, inviting, easy-going, rich, traditional spirit I've grown to love so much.

He and I had much in common. That wonderful gift of poetic expression, a devout love of our Lord and Savior, Jesus Christ, and an ultimate desire to share our words with others for enlightenment was definitely reason to sustain a long and prosperous friendship which continues to grow. Within those bounds, I witnessed a metamorphosis of epic proportions in Marc. He blossomed from a guy who wrote poetry to relieve his mind to a prolific poet, writer, and performer. I had the honor of engaging in numerous events, performances, television appearances, and just plain leisure with a man who is undoubtedly one of the best artists I've encountered in my lifetime.

When he informed me the title of his first work was to be Deeply Rooted, I felt that nothing would be more appropriate. Marc is definitely deeply rooted in his vision, his thought, his love of his race, his faith and the product of his Father, mankind. Marc Worthy is a people's man. When you meet him, you'll see his smile and feel his spirit before he opens his mouth. When he speaks, you'll be amazed. The same will be felt as you explore his thoughts through his words.

CHAPTER 1
GIVING BACK TO GOD

MARC WORTHY

DEEPLY ROOTED

*For I'm Deeply Rooted
In the word of God first,
He's like my savior in life,
As I thirst,
After peace in His word of wisdom,
Knowledge and understanding,
It takes me high up in the clouds,
And then brings me down,
To a clear landing.
The words send me,
On a plane ride so I can see,
What God has in store,
Or planned for me.
So, I want have to walk blind
Folded into suffering and pain,
When I fear Him
He opens my door,
So, I have a lot to gain.
For I'm truly Deeply Rooted
Like that pear tree,
Sprouting up from the roots
Into becoming a beautiful strong
Thing to be.
Putting a stamp on me
As well as my fruits that I bare,
Laying a hand on our life
Showing that He cares.*

DEEPLY ROOTED

Taking us on a tour of righteousness
As we grab hold to His wings,
We come together to praise Him,
Through our voices so we sing.
I'm Deeply Rooted
Like the mother bear
Taking care of her cubs,
Keeping them from harm
And spreading so much love.
Fighting off the enemies
As they lurk near,
There is always someone,
Or something in us that we fear.
I'm Deeply Rooted
In this family value thing,
It warms my heart,
To the utmost to bring,
Such wonderful children into this world,
They're more precious than diamonds,
Or the gift of pearls.
I'm so happy that I have,
Such a beautiful mother,
I thank her for having me,
And blessing me like no other.
Now that I have become,
A rare specimen in this way of life,
I put it in GOD hands,
For that search for my wife.
So, I can then put in my mind,
That I'm complete,
Summing up my life

MARC WORTHY

*It would be so unique.
I'm Deeply Rooted
In my heritage as I search for my roots,
Buckling down in these books
And my studies as I put on my boots.
Going out to find
What I feel that was deprived,
Trying to dig through this puzzle,
In hope to find facts so I can arrive,
To something that is concrete
That I can stand by,
And really don't have to ask,
The question why.
I'm Deeply Rooted
In setting these goals,
Sitting back and looking
As they all unfold.
Not to let them go
By the waste side,
Picking them up
And then taking stride,
For excellent and setting
Them very, very high,
Escalating to the top
As I complete them
And end up in the sky.
I'm Deeply Rooted
In what is supposed to be,
The American way,
U know peace, justice, and equality
In my heart it will change someday.*

DEEPLY ROOTED

Then America can be truly
The land of the free, home of the brave,
There will be no more bloodshed,
And my people can take off the cuffs,
And be saved.
Where we can come together
And hold hands and praise GOD with each other,
And look at me for
My content of character,
And not by color.
For all, of these things
I'm truly deeply, Deeply Rooted.

MARC WORTHY

FAITH

*Many people walk this earth,
Thinking why should I live
If I'm cursed.
Not having the faith within,
Walking blind folded
Into the path of sin.
Their confidence shattered,
Leaving them guessing
For a way to turn,
While the mind is screaming out
The heart is in a state of yearning.
Needing to be rescued
By this person from up above,
Hoping that they can be,
Crowded by attention and much love.
But still not finding,
The ways to be blessed,
Roads seem pitch dark,
And all they can think about
Is being depressed.
Turning up the wine bottle
Hoping to get a reply,
After its gone u are sick
And that leaves the question why.
Still not satisfied,
Needing something stronger
To fill that plug,
So, u turn for help by way of drugs.*

DEEPLY ROOTED

It's steady sucking u in close,
To the middle,
I hope u have a plan and a pillow.
Right now, u are quickly falling down,
U should have a soft landing
Before u hit the ground.
But before u come
To a crashing halt,
Picking up the Holy Bible
That would be a good thought.
Turn to the part that said,
" By grace are ye saved
Through faith,"
And that not of yourselves:
It is the gift of GOD.
Not of works,
Lest any man should boast."
Sit back on that!
And have a toast.

MARC WORTHY

MY SHADOW

*Just the other day
I thought I heard my shadow say,
"Marc, let me guide u the right way."
I looked up, down, and all around
There was my shadow on the ground.
Smiling up at me and talking,
Telling me to keep on walking.
Commenting on how
He had my back,
Especially, when I started to slack.
And if I was to fall,
That, all I had to do was call.
He would come running very quick,
Straight through the mind so it would stick.
Floating me along like a kite,
And molding me with all his might.
I always turn to him,
When I get worried,
To hear him say not to get discouraged.
He is my strong hold and my shield,
Beating down bugs at will.
Stressing that I need to start living right,
And to put him first
And foremost in my life.
That I would be commended at the end,
All I had to do was report my sins.
He always tells me to donate my,*

DEEPLY ROOTED

Time and money,
That my path will be sweeter than honey.
My shadow inspires me,
To keep a smile on my face,
No matter how much wrong takes place.
To put it in his hand,
And to let him take care of the land.
For me to keep on
Climbing the success ladder,
That's why he's, my shadow.

MARC WORTHY

MISSING U

*I see that her time has,
Come to past,
But through it all her memories
Shall it last.
In this world of suffering
And struggles of pain,
Climbing through the clouds
And entering a place with
A lot of gain.
Now she's like that bird,
Nesting in the tree,
Her heart has truly
Been delivered and set free.
For now, she can finally rest,
And let her mind roam,
Grabbing hold of the angels' wings
They will bring her home.
A lot of people have that sorrow,
That they let fill the atmosphere,
Hoping that it will bring,
Her back close and near.
Now through it all
Happiness rules the airway,
As she sits under her father
As he watches over her,
We now know,
She will really be okay.*

DEEPLY ROOTED

All that is really left are our,
Simple goodbyes,
We come together in one place,
To spread love through tears so we cry.
Goodbyes aren't,
The easiest of things,
But through it the entire lord brings,
The pure pleasure of knowing,
Such a wonderful
And beautiful woman,
But through her thoughts we share
And enjoy even if she left this land.
It's truly been an exciting experiment,
That has brought the best out in me,
She's that type of person,
If she comes in contact with u,
Her personality rubs off on u,
Keeping u warm as can be.
She had an essential
But inviting kind of smile,
Welcoming u in
Was her kind of style.
I know she's standing,
At those pearly gates,
Her name at the top of the list,
Down here without
A shadow of doubt
She will be missed.

MARC WORTHY

WHEN I THINK OF HOME

*When I think of home,
I sit back, kick my feet up,
And let my mind roam.
Thinking about the time when
I walk through those pearly gates,
I feel love in the air,
And happiness of leaving
A world full of hate.
I'm all around people,
That are full of peace,
There are no rumors of wars,
And no celebration from the beast.
No more worrying about
Diseases and people getting sick,
I'm enjoying this and hopefully,
This message will stick.
To all of u like super glue,
And just maybe u will get the clue.
From my home I will never,
Ever, have to complain about my health,
For that matter I won't have
To look into the eyes of death.
No more growling of the stomach
When I think of starvation,
Coming from the past
Of trials and tribulations.
For I have fulfilled my path*

DEEPLY ROOTED

And lived out GOD'S revelation.
Now I can take a breath of fresh air,
And feel the sensation.
Of walking down, a road
To see the buildings made of gold,
In a place where people don't age
Or think about getting old.
Home is a place,
Where everybody has fame,
U just won't see anybody
Suffering or living in pain.
The walls of my home
Are made of very rare stones,
It really brings it out,
And sets the tone.
For light to come through
Shining like a jewel,
In this home everybody rules.
There is no need for a sun or a moon,
For all, of the faithful people
Will come to this home soon.
Where the light will shine day and night,
For this home is out of sight.
So, come on and join me,
In letting your mind roam,
And let the glory of the Lord,
Bring u home.
And let the glory of the Lord,
Bring u home.

MARC WORTHY

HAVING THE LIGHT

My heart had a lot of darkness,
That came to past one night,
For I gathered my sword
And began to fight,
As I was traveling to the light.
So, I believe that I'm one
Of the children of the light,
Because it shines
Or echoes oh so bright.
For it was not always
That easy as I
Stumbled and fell,
Reaching and grabbing
The word of GOD made it well.
I was blinded by the things,
That I saw on this earth,
Thinking my life
Had already been labeled,
A curse.
Then the Lord revealed to me
In a dream,
That my life will never be made
Of peaches and cream.
I know that Satan,
Will play on my emotions,
When I'm down,
But if I truly believe

DEEPLY ROOTED

In the word of GOD
And his power,
Then Satan would go away
With a frown.
But knowing his encounters
Would be lurking near,
To see if I was going,
To crumble so he could
Whisper in my ear.
Feeding me with junk
From a long metal rod,
But the Bible tells us,
That we loved the praise of men
More than the praise of GOD.
The devil can easily
Enter through the flesh,
But if we are in the spirit
GOD will destroy his mess.
The Lord is my light,
And my salvation
Whom shall, I fear?
He's the strength of my life,
Because He's always near.
Entering through
The heart and the mind,
Teaching me discipline
So, my reaction
Will be swift and kind.
Glowing every minute
As I walk oh so proud,
It feels as if I'm floating along,

MARC WORTHY

And lighting up the clouds.
Carrying me on his shoulder
To the correct way,
GOD is forever in me,
Where He's going to stay.

DEEPLY ROOTED

LIFE OF SIN

*Hey GOD,
I'm ready to come home,
Trying to show u,
That, this is where I belong.
Ready to escape,
This way of sin,
So tired of running ready,
To put this to an end.
I know u can hear me calling,
The devil got me tied up,
And I'm slowly falling.
For I'm truly at my worst
At this point in my lifetime,
I'm hoping and praying,
That u can be hard but kind.
U said that if I confess
With my mouth
And believe in thine heart,
That thou shalt be saved
And that will be my start.
For I'm so used to having
These evil ways,
That I'm steady
Counting my days.
When I can sprout wings
Out of my back and fly,
And meet with u,*

MARC WORTHY

In that great heavenly sky.
We can sit down at the table,
And have bread and wine,
Think of all the ways
That we can possibly fine.
To nurture and bring
To all the truth,
Spreading the word
Especially to the youth.
So that they can have
A long and prosperous road,
And u can look over them,
And watch their life unfold.
So, they can go out,
And give good tidings,
And bring more sinners,
Out of hiding.
Now we must keep fighting,
And doing away with pain,
As he builds this gospel chain.

DEEPLY ROOTED

JESUS HELP

Here I am such a vulnerable man,
Satan plays with my emotions,
I need Jesus to hold my hands.
Guide and mold me ever so tight,
He talks to me,
In my prayers at night.
He picks me up and carries me,
From the darkness to light,
He gives me the power,
And wisdom to fight.
I need to keep hearing your voice,
Telling me what's right,
So, I can build confidence,
And not lose sight.
U know that Satan
Has a way with his tongue,
He tries to enter my head,
And get me sprung.
It's as if he trying to brain wash me,
Or cover up my eyes,
So that I can't see.
I know that I have to be,
Strong against Satan
Who is very deceptive,
And loves to turn the truth around,
I need u Jesus to purify my heart,
So, I won't stay down.

MARC WORTHY

Just lend me your helping arm,
To fight off the beast
That only cares about doing me harm.
Keep reminding me of the Bible,
Being my shield,
As I study, the word keeps me from getting ill.
I know that Satan is down below,
Feeling mighty sick,
As I cling onto u Jesus as my top pick.
I know he won't give up that easy on me,
But I'll come prepared as can be.
As I fight him off by reading my sword,
And standing by Jesus
For we are on one accord.
Now Satan u can't even
Come close enough to measure,
That's why I give Jesus all the pleasure.
Now I'm waiting for my reward at the end,
For I know that I was forgiven for my past sins.

DEEPLY ROOTED

MARC WORTHY

ONE FLESH

The coming together
Of two beautiful hearts,
Dancing and smiling all the way,
From the very start.
As we grab hold to the wings
From the man up above,
He guides and nurtures,
To us the meaning of love.
Today will be the beginning,
Of our biggest test,
As husband and wife
Comes together as
One flesh.
Leaving their father and their mother,
And shall cleave on to each other.
Listening to the awesome sounds
Of the birds,
As the preacher brings forth
These special words.
People in the audience
Are quiet as a mouse,
As they are hearing
These powerful words rock the house.
But before the preacher
Start to dismiss,
He tells us to seal the deal,
With one big kiss.

DEEPLY ROOTED

After we do this
Is where the show me time begins,
Satan comes in effect,
Trying to cause us to sin.
Because in every marriage
There are going to be some problems,
But u have to remember,
We are as
One flesh
And we both have to come together,
To solve them.
Satan will really try,
To stir things up
By playing with both of our minds,
But remembering our creator's words
We shall be fine.
Not saying that this won't be hard,
But we must be stern,
Joining each other hands
On holy grounds we stand firm.
So, come on Satan
Take your best shots,
GOD protects us,
As we tie this knot.
For we are ready
To weather all
The storms and tests,
This family is ready,
To be truly blessed.

MARC WORTHY

NO JUSTICE IN MAN

For deep down
In my soul I thirst,
When man can rely
On GOD'S commandments,
And listen to
His instructions first.
When two Christ like men
Come together,
To work out their problems,
Where they don't need
Man, to come together,
To solve them.
What I mean
Is a person shouldn't,
Have to go to court,
To be heard,
Especially if they are,
Into the Lord's word.
Why should I put my problems,
Into the hands
Of a lot of unbelievers?
For the system is ran
By greedy people and deceivers.
Why should we,
As brothers let man
Choose our fate?
Not knowing the outcome

DEEPLY ROOTED

*Is a downright mistake.
Most of the system
Is run by slanderers, swindlers, and crooks,
That's how most of the GOD'S fairing people,
Often gets mistook.
Often, they get used and abused,
As Satan finds a way
To use the system
As a get even tool.
For our body is like
A temple that Satan tries to deploy,
But if we are both
following the Lord's ways,
Satan shouldn't be able,
To come in between and destroy.
What I mean
Is that we as Christians,
Should be able to talk,
Man to man,
Work out our problems,
According to the Lord's plan.
If we can't seem to work, it out
Take the problem to a preacher,
Let him be our mentor or our teacher.
If u still aren't satisfied
With the outcome or situation,
The word teaches us to be patient.
So, don't get down,
Like a frog needing a pod,
Just remember that,
The wicked will not inherit,*

MARC WORTHY

The kingdom of GOD.

DEEPLY ROOTED

SMILE

Here we go all over again,
Can u please stop and grin?
A smile a day,
Might keep all the bad people away.
I smile a lot to let people know,
The happiness I have inside,
It carries about ten feet long,
And ten feet wide.
They tell me that I look like
The man on the Kool-Aid pack,
That's okay because GOD,
Gives me great pleasure,
And I give him the glory back.
He instilled in me that things,
Aren't always going to go my way,
But if I keep open minded
And continue to stay focused,
That it will work out for the very best,
To hold on too morals in good spirit
And let him take care of the rest.
For I feel so jolly and radiant
From deep down in my soul,
That my body just beams
It's not being arrogant or bold.
It's the beauty within
That I just have to let it out,
It's that seed that the Lord has planted,

MARC WORTHY

*That has begun to sprout.
Yielding fruit that is better
Than the touch of pure gold,
And riches and honors
Are with me as the story is told.
U know people tell me that
I have this glow about myself,
That my inner self-shining from far off
Showing GOD keeps me in great health.
For he tells us to acknowledge him
And he shall direct our paths,
That our days will be filled
With rejoicing and much laughs.
To keep his commandments
That our length of days would be long
And in peace,
He will build this wall to stop,
Or confuse the beast.
For happiness is something
That I can be proud of that was shown,
It's health to the navel,
And marrow to the bones.
The word said, "happy,
Is the man that found wisdom,
And the man who perceive understanding,"
U should be able to follow
The instructions for it's not too demanding.
Let your heart and mind,
Have the right to be set free,
And showing your smile
Is the essential key.*

DEEPLY ROOTED

So, when u are at an agreement
Or content as can be,
Show them pretty whites,
So, the world can see.
"Smile"

MARC WORTHY

TEMPTATION

*I often stare at the sky and wonder,
How life is slowly trying to take me under.
See it's like my feet are stuck in quicksand,
And they are trying to suck me off this land.
I keep fighting them off with lefts and rights,
But Satan keeps throwing them,
At me with all his might.
He has me in agony, so he smiles,
But I keep praying to GOD all the while.
Asking him to deliver me from
All the pain and the mess,
To spare my heart from all the stress.
For now, they have me
Wrapped up in this cocoon,
So, I'm calling for some help,
Because I'm a goner soon.
They got me mesmerized,
By the way they walk.
Tranquilizing me with
The way they talk.
Putting me under a spell
With their looks and smells.
Will someone please ring that darn bell?
Bring me back to this place we call earth,
They had me trapped in hell since birth.
Got me singing out for their attention.
Telling me to stay silent and not to mention.*

DEEPLY ROOTED

A word to the man from up above,
Who will strengthen me,
Through the power of love!
Take most of my temptations of women away,
And place one woman
In my path to my final day.
He's got me lined up with my other half,
Calling on him will make our love last.
I've defeated the beast again,
That's right it's over my friends.
GOD is the winner once again,
For he was with me to the very end.

MARC WORTHY

THE MAN THAT I CAN BE

For I'm startled by
The way that I can be,
For it's the man that is in me.
Like I'm the volcano
And the devil is the fire,
He tried to burn me down but
My soul lifted me higher.
Through all the turmoil
And chaos I remain,
The mountain that stands,
Through all the pain.
He builds and molds,
His willpower to be,
For it's the man that is in me.
The blessing that I have found,
That keeps me standing,
On solid ground.
It leaves the beast,
Puzzled and in shame,
While my hands are raised
At the end of the game.
For I'm startled by
The way that I can be,
For it's the man that is in me.
That keeps me prepared.
For his return,
He's not done,

DEEPLY ROOTED

As the world turns.
U know the devil has tricky
And conniving ways,
But in my mind
My confidence stays,
So, I put on my battle uniform,
And look him in the eye,
And battle with him
Until the day I die.
When I'm gone, I leave knowing,
I've done my best,
And when I reach heaven
And shake GOD'S hands,
I know I've passed the test.
For I'm startled by
The way that I can be,
For it's the man that is in me.

MARC WORTHY

PILLAR IN THE CHURCH

*Passing away of a loved one
Is always trying,
To say she was like
A pillar in the church
Brings me to crying.
She has gone away,
But her presence has been felt,
Especially in church
All the kids she kept.
She always had something,
To do to keep their attention,
She also played nurse,
To the sick I must mention.
When the pastor needed water
She was always there,
It was her duty to do good,
Because she cares.
I just feel like church,
Couldn't function without her around,
She kept everything glued,
And from falling down.
If church started at nine,
She would be there at eight,
I can't remember a time,
When she was ever late.
In Morning Service
She would be the first,*

DEEPLY ROOTED

To lead a song,
And boy I say,
That lady could hum.
As she would sing
The drummer continued to beat,
She could bring,
The church to their feet.
They would clap and cheer,
It seems that she brought,
The whole church close and near.
In Sunday school
It was no problem for her,
To lend a hand to teach,
If the pastor was not going to be around
She could also preach.
I can recall like it was yesterday,
She would begin and end with a prayer,
Many of the church people
Would be amazed and some would stare.
They were waiting for her to fail,
Or to lack,
So, they could run and tell,
The pastor when he came back.
But she was very precise,
And so very firm,
Her voice came down,
Hard and stern.
When the pastor was back to preach
She would help pass the tray around,
She did all this with a smile,
She never wore a frown.

MARC WORTHY

When the church was planning
To go on the road to sing,
She was there to help bring,
Along the support needed
To carry them through,
She always brought along her crew.
The church could always
Count on her being on their list,
Now that she's gone,
She will be truly missed.
The services' she rendered,
Is what's going to hurt,
For she was a
Pillar in the church.

DEEPLY ROOTED

BRING ON THE FIRE

Here I am living around,
Crooked politicians and a bunch
Of non-believing people,
GOD said there's nothing new,
Under the sun and that
It's an ongoing sequel.
People today are falling,
In the same path as the Israelites did,
They stop believing,
And going against what GOD forbid.
Always questioning
His ways and his thoughts,
To them it came to a punishing halt.
Not letting them enter
Into the land of milk and honey,
They wondered around for about,
Forty years in the wilderness,
Because they tested GOD
Now isn't that funny.
Our problems today are about the same,
We should have learned,
From the Israelites stupid shame.
So, I say to the person up higher,
U need to bring on the fire.
Show these non-believers,
What is now at hand,
Let it rain down upon them,

MARC WORTHY

So, they can better understand.
U are the Alpha and the Omega,
The beginning and the end,
Those that don't believe,
Will be destroyed because they've sinned.
For those who chose to live
Under Satan regulation,
U better first turn
To the book of Revelation.
Get knowledgeable before
GOD makes his way down here,
But if u still don't comprehend
The truth you better fear,
So, I say to the person up higher,
U need to bring on the fire.
GOD is the first, the source of all creation,
He is also the last,
Standing at the end of time.
Pick up the Bible,
And read so u won't be left in the blind.
He's coming to do away,
With all things that Satan
Has brought here,
If u didn't get it, he will make it clear.
All u high paid people
At the top making decisions
To bring on war,
U need to think twice,
What you are really asking for.
War will bring upon many,
Of the problems at hand,

DEEPLY ROOTED

*For the simple-minded people
Still don't seem to understand.
So, I say to the person up higher,
U need to bring on the fire.
Make them see that war,
Brings about bad things,
Such as starvation, sorrow, and death,
If we have this next war
There will probably be no one left.
I pray that this won't come about,
For we have enough problems with diseases,
We need to wake up,
And come together to seize this.
If we don't I say to the person up higher,
U need to bring on the fire.
I don't want to be around for this,
Can u please take me away,
So, I can find my name on that list?
That will enter me into
This beautiful New World,
Where the walls are made
Of precious stones and buildings
Are made of gold,
I can sit back and rest my soul,
And won't have to worry about getting old,
And for all the people that didn't believe,
I think GOD has been patient indeed.
So, I say to the person up higher,
Go ahead and
Bring on the fire!*

MARC WORTHY

DEEPLY ROOTED

WALK, STAND, SIT

One day I was on
The basketball court-playing ball,
I heard this unusual voice,
Squeak out a call.
There was no one around,
But this old looking man,
He was sitting on the bench,
And feeding the birds
Out of his hands.
He came up to the court,
With this funny looking grin,
He told me that GOD had told him,
To come because I was living in sin.
So, I kept shooting,
And running after my ball,
Not really paying attention
To this man at all.
He kept on saying,
That one day I would truly be blessed,
Not thinking that this might be,
GOD'S way of putting me through a test.
So, I spoke and told,
The old man to let it be,
The man kept speaking,
And calls out my name,
Like he had known me.
I just stopped in my tracks,

MARC WORTHY

And gave him this confused stare,
He peeped back,
And said yes GOD cares.
Then he asked me
If we could take a short walk,
I said yes and he began to talk.
The more he talked the more I heard,
This loud chirping sound,
Coming from the mouth of a bird.
I kept listening to the bird chirping,
And gazing up to the sky.
The old man kept talking,
It felt like time had passed me by.
I found myself,
Standing by the bench
With the old man,
It seems like we traveled miles,
Because my shoe was covered with sand.
He told me if I believe in GOD,
And his righteousness that the shoes would last.
That it wouldn't seem like
I travel so far if I took His path.
The old man kept talking about
The ungodly shall perish someday,
And that I would have to choose
Or my blessing would fade away.
I listened to the old man so much,
And he kept hitting, all the points in my life,
That was bad that I found myself sitting.
Looking upward and meditating
So long that the day turn to night,

DEEPLY ROOTED

When I came down
The old man was nowhere in sight.
My mind was at a standstill,
With nowhere to roam,
As I sat there it felt like
I was finally at home.

MARC WORTHY

CHAPTER 2
ALL ABOUT LOVE

DEEPLY ROOTED

Love Spell

*Being in love
Gives me the cheers,
It helps me,
Fight back those tears.
I feel like love is happiness,
That has been bolstered,
Emotions running high,
And low like a roller coaster.
Soft and sweet words,
That are whispered through the air,
I enjoy the passion,
When you stop, and you stare.
The look in your eyes,
Tell me to be aware,
Your calm and cool demeaner,
Shows me you care.
Temptation lingers,
Here and there.
Your mind,
Combined with your body,
I just can't bare,
I melt like Jello,
In the mouth,
Over your long and gorgeous hair.
And your lips,
Oow, your lips,
Forever, tear me up all inside,
And your sense of humor,*

MARC WORTHY

Takes me for a ride.
Come on,
And embrace me girl,
Trap me,
In "YOUR WORLD."
Hold me for ransom,
Without a fee,
Love me forever,
And throw away the key.
Let's have a toast,
So, grab your mug,
You got me going Crazy,
With those warm hugs.
Your love,
Takes me under, so deep,
Temperatures soars high,
Emotions,
Are running steep.
I haven't learned,
My lesson,
When you rub,
Up against me,
You can feel the erection.
This is a true conception,
How this perception,
Takes over the body,
Uncontrollable urges,
Makes me become naughty.
When you leave,
From around,
It feels like,

DEEPLY ROOTED

It takes me,
A whole "month" to calm down.
See your love is all well,
You got me hearing,
"Wedding Bells."
Even though,
You left me soaking,
Under your Spell,
"Love Spell"

MARC WORTHY

LOVE ONE ANOTHER

*People today they really
Don't care for one another,
They need to learn how,
To give love out to each other.
It seems to me,
When u are trying to prosper and grow,
There is always someone,
There to try to stop your flow.
Always there to hate.
Or say things that is a put down,
But when u succeed
They are the first ones,
To come around.
Smiling in your face,
But u feel that envy on your back,
U still try to play it off
By cutting them some slack.
In reality if u had listened
To what they had to say,
U wouldn't be where u are today.
Trying to knock u off
From your true blessing,
Trying to keep u where they are,
By tampering and messing.
U need to tell them what got,
U there more than twice,
Hopefully they will catch on
To the sign and put Jesus in their life.*

DEEPLY ROOTED

For the fear of the Lord
Is to hate evil, arrogance, and pride,
We should also remember,
To pay our tithes.
That's the clue,
To getting fruitful and rich,
In Jesus eyes
That's a home run hit not a miss.
He tells us that "I love them that love me,"
And "those that seek me early shall find me."
That should open the door,
For those who fail to see.
So, u see there is no reason to hate,
All u have to do is to also have faith.
Then u can increase your wealth
That will continue to grow,
And just maybe there is a pot of gold,
At the end of the rainbow.

MARC WORTHY

DEFINING THE WORD LOVE

*I have learned to live life,
For what it's worth,
Through Adam we must live
It in a curse.
There are times when we must,
Go through all sorts of pain,
But through it all we will gain,
Three things that will last forever and ever,
These things are faith, hope,
And love will always be used cleverly.
I think the most important,
One of these is the word love,
It's such a small word,
That hovers over my head
Like a handsome dove.
Love is a word that is used,
Over and over and never gets old,
U can say it soft and sweet
Or u can say it bold.
Love is a word that conquers all things,
It comes from the heart, so it brings,
Upon happiness and peace
Throughout the land.
For that was supposed to be the plan.
Love is awesome and so very kind,
Sometimes it's the hardest thing to find.
So, I say with a stern mouth,
Patience is the way to go,*

DEEPLY ROOTED

*Through the word of GOD
Or a soul mate I say open the door.
It comes about in all shape and forms,
For it's a word that is used
To warm up the spirit,
So, take it with u and run away,
Place it in your life for that final day.
Because in a world
Full of the word hate,
I find love as a way to escape,
Rude and unbarring people
That crosses my trail,
Selfish people please come from
Under Satan's spell.
Grab hold to love for its calling,
It will stop all good men from falling.
Seek the word of GOD for yourself,
His love will keep u in sound health.
So, I pray, and I pray,
For that memorable day,
When love takes over
This land to stay.*

MARC WORTHY

IT COULD HAVE BEEN ME

It could have been me,
For I was out there, u see.
I was caught up in the streets.
Trying to get with
Every girl I meet.
I thought that having,
A lot of women was pleasing,
I was very lucky,
To have escaped
Those many diseases.
I know that it wasn't,
For the best,
But I felt like it was a test,
It stemmed from not having,
The knowledge within.
Sometimes, it takes a while,
To learn from your sins.
It could have been me,
For I was caught up
In the game u see.
I could have easily
Been caught using drugs,
Or on the corner trying
To be a thug.
For it was the way to go
In the hood,
It was all I saw,
So therefore, I thought,
It was good.

DEEPLY ROOTED

My mother got caught up,
In those fine lines,
Using and abusing drugs
From time to time.
So, I used her mistakes,
To find a way to bail,
Or I would have probably
Ended up in jail.
Now I take time,
To go that extra mile,
To speak against
This awful lifestyle.
It could have been me,
I could have been,
A thief u see.
Though I always had
The proper food,
I used to steal because,
I thought it was so cool.
I used to go into stores,
And try on clothes,
And if they fit,
I used to debate on taking it.
I thought stealing,
Was the way,
To becoming a Mack.
I formed this opinion,
From the knowledge I lacked.
It could have been me,
For I used to try
Skipping church u see.

MARC WORTHY

I didn't have the best of clothes,
So, people picked,
So, when my grandmother
Used to wake me up,
I played sick.
She caught on,
To the matter at hand,
So, I had to think,
Of another plan.
So, I began to make my,
Head hurt,
So, I began to weep.
I cried so hard that I thought,
I could go back to sleep.
But she made me,
Go to church anyway,
She was determined that I
Was going to be in church,
On Sundays.
She taught me,
A real good lesson,
For I was about to
Miss my blessings.
So, it could have been me,
But GOD was always,
With me u see.

DEEPLY ROOTED

Silent Friend

I can hear him speak,
Although he is silent,
He speaks not a word,
But I can understand him.
He uses his hands,
And body in gestures,
So, he can express himself better.
When I'm talking
He looks at me as though,
I'm a stranger,
For really, he is reading my lips.
He's special in his own right,
But like to be treated,
As a normal person.
He can't hear this poem,
But still, he is my silent friend.

MARC WORTHY

TEDDY BEAR

Please wake up and be aware,
I would like for u to be my teddy bear.
Someone who I can hold really tight,
Especially cuddling throughout the night.
U is so fluffy and fine,
An exceptional bear who is so kind.
Every day I see u I shine.
Someday I hope to make u mine.
For u have that bow about your legs,
That can make a man,
Become humble or even beg.
For temptation is always there,
People go crazy over your long and curly hair.
So, I have to tell them to be aware,
For u are my cute teddy bear.
With your long and lasting smile,
Showing them your happiness,
Which is going to be there for a while.
I hear people talking about
How u are so charming,
And that your cheeks
Are so rosy and alarming.
I can only look and grin,
If people witness that
They should see the beauty within.
Where should I start?
How u just have your way
With warming the heart.

DEEPLY ROOTED

*Or with your soft sexy appeal,
U really makes me feel,
That I'm the only person on this earth,
Have I known u since birth?
Sometimes I get u mixed up with a dove,
Your attractiveness blocks
My mind along with your love.
U are my sweet little teddy bear,
I want to have u under my care.
So, I can rub your back,
Take over some things that u lack.
I just need to know what makes u tick,
I will also help u when u are sick.
So, all u people trying to hate or stare,
Don't worry for this is my cute
Teddy bear.*

MARC WORTHY

Tickle Yo' Ribs

*Girl, what would I give
If you would just let me,
Tickle Yo' Ribs.
I must confess girl
I'm caught up in Yo' hype
Looking at your body,
That is real tight.
And ow, girl
It's Yo' World.
And I just wanna,
Live in it for a while,
You had me won
With that sneaky smile.
And I just got to sit back
And give you this
Yes, nod.
Scoping out
That beautiful bod.
And by the way,
It really was a pleasure,
Seeing you today.
That strut across the room,
Until, that smell,
Of seductive perfume.
Took me by surprise
Like an assassin,
Could this aroma be
PASSION!*

DEEPLY ROOTED

That keeps us going
All through the night,
And reeling
All through the light.
Girl, what would I give,
If you would just let me
Tickle Yo' Ribs.
The kiss of those sexy lips
The hug onto those bodacious hips,
Looking into your eyes
Got me about to flip.
And I gotta grab hold
To this relationship.
My mind begins to linger
It might be slipping,
Through my fingers.
And it's really not fair
Do you know how much I care?
I vision us sharing a cone of ice cream,
Just before my mother,
Interrupted this dream.
Though it may seem
We was about to have a fling.
So, girl, I would love to feel
That this is real,
We only have one life to live.
What would I give,
If you would only let me
"Tickle Yo Ribs."

MARC WORTHY

A BORING DAY

*Just sitting here
With nothing
To do,
But in hopes
Of seeing you.
In my dreams,
I think of all
The nice things,
That we had.
Hoping that it
Will always last.
My life is so
Very dull,
Even though
I'm in love.
With you, is all
I think about
So much until it
Makes me shout.
Seeing you is
A pleasant view,
It really makes me
Want to comfort you
A little rub around,
So, we could
Really get down.
Me and you walking
Hand and hand,*

DEEPLY ROOTED

So, we could make
Our love stand.
Then I can
Be glad to say,
I would go down
Your path any day.

MARC WORTHY

THE PACKAGE

*Girl, u are a dime piece
From head to toe.
When u walk or strut
I see that glow.
Body shaped and curved
Like an hourglass in the light.
I was wondering how
U kept that body so tight.
Chest compared to
Most be overflowing,
Trying to keep a brother
Like me from knowing.
Stomach and hips
Tucked way in,
Looking at u
Makes a person want to sin.
Thighs thick to the point
Of no return,
You are smart with it
And so very stern.
But those legs
Are so clean-cut,
I guess that's what brings
That walk out so much.
Feet and hands
Are soft and they entice,
All I can say is that's nice!
Lips look so fluffy and wet,*

DEEPLY ROOTED

*I've not been given
A chance to kiss them yet.
Not taking away from
Your body but your mind,
After talking with u it really shines.
When u put the two together
With your heart,
That man was doomed
From the very start.
Last thing but not the least,
She gives all the credit
To GOD and not the beast.*

MARC WORTHY

A RARE FIND

Many people tell me that
I have one of the sweetest grapes
On the vine,
Not to let it go
Because it's hard to find.
To capture her heart
Or at least try to lock her down,
Because she is like a piece of treasure
That I'm glad I found.
Her smile is worth
More than a million bucks,
And when she comes around
Her presence brings me good luck.
Her spirit reveals
That she is good as gold,
I speak on this
So, the truth can be told.
She has this glow about her
When she stands and talks,
U can tell she leans on GOD
As a crutch when she walks.
She has that sway in her body
To the entire notion?
The look of happiness
Tells me that she has this magic potion.
She has this grin on her face
When we converse about seeking our goals,
Grabbing hold of each other

DEEPLY ROOTED

And watching them unfold.
She always speaks very highly
And never frowns,
And her politeness touches all
Who seem to come around.
She doesn't have many (if any)
That she calls friends,
None of them are there
When she needs them at the end.
She feels that the Lord
And me is all she, needs,
So, when we come together,
And we can feed,
Each other's thoughts and ways,
So, we can stay merry all of our livelong days.
She's all that I could envision as my soul mate.
The devil can't stand
To see us like this, so he tries to hate.
He gloats at our every move to succeed,
But thanks to this whirlwind from GOD
We have hope indeed.
Sweeping my half and her half together,
We are complete.
With this transformation
We can then delete,
All this turmoil
And these negative waves,
We have come together
And we have been saved.
Our coming together
Was destined from up high,

MARC WORTHY

And we are going to be together
'Til we die.

DEEPLY ROOTED

GODS CHILD

*Mirror; Mirror on the wall,
Who's that woman?
Standing broad shoulder and all?
Her bulk of a body
Stood out like a fresh clean day,
She smells so good
That her perfume stays with u
A mile away.
She rarely says anything
She's as quiet as a mouse,
But when she talks
Her voice rock the house.
She's very mature for her age,
And she's a church going woman
Who's saved.
She used to sit back
And judge the man
And say he was to blame,
She grew up and got hipped
To their game.
Now they have to come
In front of GOD for their test,
If they past he lay hands on them
So, they will be blessed.
She is very smart and so very cute,
If u saw her
U wouldn't dispute.
She comes about like*

MARC WORTHY

This angel in the sky,
She's so humble
And sweet and she's very shy.
Her heart is as pure
As the white snow on the ground,
She speaks nothing out
Of her mouth
But pleasant sounds.
She loves to go shopping
And read romantic books,
By the way she's
An excellent cook.
When that right man
Comes her way,
He's going to be there
Until his dying day.
She brings happiness
In a room that is down,
And smiles to all who frown.
She seem to have this appeal
On all people she meets,
Especially those strangers
She comes in contact with
On the street.
U can tell she is one of
GOD'S children,
And she's going to be
Around a long, long while.

DEEPLY ROOTED

TIME TO SHINE

Living through this
Test of time,
Now it's my time to shine.
Weathering this storm
From the front and back,
Leaning on the word
To show me things that I lack.
All this while,
I have been called,
A problem child.
Always wanting to do
Things my way,
And telling everybody
Things are going to be okay.
Still in my heart today,
I'm stubborn on the things I say.
That's just the way it is,
And not always will be.
GOD is starting
To make it clear to me.
For I used to be
Hard and demanding,
Until I read the word,
And it tells me not to lean on
My own understanding,
So, I'm really giving this
A chance to take over,
I feel protected

MARC WORTHY

And I won't have to look,
Around my shoulder.
For the Bible is
My sword and my shield,
Following his commandments
Especially
"Thou shall not kill."
Now my heart is filled
With the Holy Ghost,
And nothing else can come close.
For I'm living out my destination,
As I go through
Trials and tribulations.
For my good has really
Out shadowed my bad,
Leaving all this hatred alone
And no longer sad.
For it's my time to shine,
As I stand this
Test of time.

CHAPTER 3
HURT

MARC WORTHY

WISHING

Have u ever wished
That a man could be
So simple and real.
He could make your heart feel,
So wonderful and full of love.
Like those pretty white doves,
Descending oh so high in the air.
Like your cute sexy hair.
U are so elegant and timid
I shall say,
My regard for u is in the heart
Where it shall stay!
U got me
Dancing and prancing
In the clouds causing it to rain,
I have no shame in my game.
Especially when it comes to u
And the way I feel,
I can't express how real.
I can only show u
In a matter of time,
Hoping that someday
You could be mine.
When my heart connects
With your heart,
Then it becomes a start.
For us as a couple to enjoy life,
Never to think twice.

DEEPLY ROOTED

I'm a man of ambition,
Hoping I can reward u
Of all your wishes.
Your wants and desire,
Will only cause us to aim higher.
Come on and take my hand,
And let GOD lead us
To the promise land.
He's like that supporting cast,
Leaning on him will make our love last.
I'm forever indebted in u.
Because I will always love u.
We should be ready to take that next step,
For we really have some help.
With GOD being our tour guide,
It could be a fun, filled ride.
Straight to the top of ever,
Ever land and that is our plan.
As u can see, I need u
To complete me.

DEEPLY ROOTED

SO COLD

U are so cold,
I hope u have a change of mind,
And someday u could be kind.
I say u are as cold as a refrigerator,
Lips wicked like the terminator,
U don't care about no one but yourself,
If it's not your problem
U put it away on the shelf.
Always thinking it's not me,
Not thinking one day it could be.
So, I say again u are so cold,
I hope u have a change of mind,
And some day u could be kind.
U always find a way
To not help your peers,
It's a shame u rather see
Them come to tears.
Talking about they should
Have planned on the situation,
Instead of sitting back and being patient.
Keeping your thoughts
And all your money to yourself,
Hoping that will be enough
To keep u in good health.
U are so arrogant and so very cocky,
Walking around with your hands
All in your pocket.
Praying that someone will ask u

MARC WORTHY

For some of that money,
So, u can start laughing
And look at them funny.
U are so cold,
I hope u have a change of mind,
And some day u could be kind.
Walking around with a frown
Upon your face,
Having too much power
And don't know how to control it,
What a disgrace.
Slowly u find yourself
Down deep in the pits,
Trying to keep count of your funds
But can't calculate all of it.
IRS and others are now
Putting their hands in the matter,
I hope that u have a big ladder.
Or hopefully u put some money up
For a rainy day,
If u didn't then u are really going to pay.
Now don't u wish that u had a heart of gold?
Instead, u had to be so, so cold.
I know now that u will
Have a change of mind,
And that the outcome will be kind.

DEEPLY ROOTED

DANGEROUS GAME

Girl, u are playing
This dangerous game,
For your heart should
Be full of shame.
Talking about u want to be
With me but marry to my friend,
That is just another way
To have my blessing done in.
I can't believe u are calling me
And telling me things like this,
U should be talking to your husband
Whether it's a hit or a miss.
U better hope he don't
Open up his eyes to see,
That u are trying to go
Behind his back and talk to me.
What ever happened to those words?
That u said to one another.
I guess u just swept them under the cover.
For u both need to come together
And get in tune with Christ.
Then he can put the pieces
In place for u both, to start living right.
U must remember that
We all have faults and ways,
U both need to overcome them
So that u can prosper all your livelong days.
U need to pay more attention to him

MARC WORTHY

And leave me alone,
For he is going to slip away
And be long gone.
And for me
I already have found me a wife,
So, you're better off staying put
And putting me out of your life.
That's my friend
I could never cross his path,
For our friendship will forever last.
I feel like
If u don't want to be with him
Let him go,
Because u have already
Under cut him by going low.
Here u are trying to call me
All time of the night,
And trying to dodge me
When he comes in sight.
I was trying not to
Tell him the situation,
I'm trying to let it
Flow over by being patient.
I'm saying this with all thou soul,
U need to stay with your husband
So, your blessing will
Be back tenfold.
U can then stop playing
This dangerous game,
And love your husband
And put away the shame.

DEEPLY ROOTED

HURT

*Can we please sit down,
Long enough to talk?
I can remember when
We took long walks.
Holding each other's hand
And gazing in each other's eyes,
Those were the days
I have to say my, my, my.
Conversing over problems
And things of that matter,
It kept our relationship
From becoming unraveled.
Dealing with those
Bad dilemmas
Like woman to man,
Taking care of those
Issues hand in hand.
Now u are so cold hearted
And don't even care,
Standing around with your head
All in the air.
Not answering your phone
And acting very bold,
I guess someone else
Is there wiping your nose.
I put up with this mess*

MARC WORTHY

For a few years,
All I've gotten from this
Is headaches and tears.
Tried to reveal to u
That u was one of a kind.
Taking u for
A night on the town
Wine and dine.
Spoiling u with love
And material things,
Not to mention,
Giving u all of my,
Undivided attention.
And when u were down
Or sick lying-in bed,
There I was making sure u smile
And, that u was fed.
Showering u with surprise gifts
At your work,
While u gave me
All this verbal abuse that hurt.
Doing things that
Were not so cool,
Here I am putting u
On this pedestal.
Listening to u complain about
You're many concerns,
Putting the pieces together
To make our relationship firm.
U still wasn't satisfied
So, I have to let u go,

DEEPLY ROOTED

Especially when I caught u
Creeping out my back door.
Going to see my neighbor
And probably a lot more men,
Getting hung up, you saying
They are just my friends.
Now I see that u want
To ring my phone,
Telling me to come over
That u are all alone.
They must have left u
High and dry,
So, can I ask u?
The question why would
A woman goes out and lust,
When they have a man
Who cares about them so much?
I know it is about the word "Greed",
The grass is greener
When u plant that seed.
I see that
U are miserable and down,
U better pray
That another good man
Comes around.

MARC WORTHY

TELL ME IF U CARE

I know that I wasn't always there,
But can u tell me that u still care?
I have been in and out of your life,
It's been ten years
And I haven't made u my wife.
Leaving u time after time again,
Most of them were flings with your friends.
After a while they would tell u,
I would make some kind
Of excuse that wasn't true.
In your mind u knew it was a lie,
U loved me so u never asked me why.
I really think u were afraid to ask me
Because I would get mad,
Start to curse u out.
That's sad.
Looking back that wasn't
The biggest thing that hurt,
Not being a man
And watching u go to work.
At that moment I thought
It was kind of funny,
U would work hard
While I spend all the money.
I used to take u for granted
As if u were a joke,
Now I can only sit back and hope.
For I know that I wasn't always there,

DEEPLY ROOTED

But can u tell me that u still care?
Since the last time we've been apart
I've grown-up from the games,
I'm so sorry for calling u
All those disrespectful names.
I have to give u the credit for
Turning me from a boy to a man,
So, I hope u find it in your heart
To forgive me if u can.
For I have been crying the blues,
I don't know what to do,
I'm simply lost without u.
I've really been on the out,
Since u left, I've been
Staring at the walls in this lonely house.
For I know that I wasn't always there,
But can u tell me if u still care?
I know that I've made this
A very hard decision,
But lately I've been seeing this vision.
U and I all the while,
Kissing and embracing
After we walked down that aisle.
I'm ready to man up to my responsibility,
In taking care of u, u see.
For I know I wasn't always there,
So, just tell me if u still care.

MARC WORTHY

BLESSING BLOCKER

*It's time for class
To be in session,
All u beautiful women
Need to take my lesson.
On these bad men
Who is a blessing blocker,
So, get your note pad
And pen out of your locker.
Report to my room
As fast as u can
Like on the double,
I have some good news
That just might keep
U out of trouble.
If u have a lot of pride
Please don't come here,
What I have to say
Won't be pleasant my dear.
For most of u women
Are looking for a man
For the wrong reason,
Because u are lonely
And u think he can help u
Bring in the season.
For loneliness is from
The state of the mind,
Basing it on that,
U Will find yourself in a bind.*

DEEPLY ROOTED

I hope that u are still taking notes
On these blessing blockers,
For when I get through
I hope my words
Knock u off your rockers.
For women u need
To get hip to these men
Talk games,
For they are all around
The same line and are so lame.
Saying things like
"Baby I want to be with u forever,"
U don't even know me,
For that wasn't even clever.
Another way these men come at u
Is by waving their funds,
For most of u women
Who will fall for this
I say stick to your guns.
They see that u are in need
Of some things,
They prey upon that,
Hoping that it will bring,
Them what they are really
Looking for,
So, I say please slam that door.
Tell that man u are worth more
Then the value of money,
Not to throw that up
In your face, honey.
Another way women

MARC WORTHY

*Have their blessings blocked,
They feel like they have to lie
In a man's arms around the clock.
All u women need to sit down
And relate,
So, u won't be just another
Statue in his trophy case.
U will then feel used
And abused,
Before long that man
Will have u confused.
For u won't know
Which way to turn,
That's why u must
Stay stern.
Especially by the way
Of the heart,
That will be a good place
To start.
Tell that man
To get rid of all that
Which is above,
To leave u alone
If he's not in it for love.
For that is how a man
And woman should flow,
That's how they can prosper and grow.
Through the power of love
Is how a man should jock her,
That will get rid of her
Blessing blockers.*

DEEPLY ROOTED

PAPER-THIN

I thought that u were my friend,
But now I see your heart is paper-thin.
See I've known u since we were boys,
Going over each other's house
And playing with each other's toys.
We grew up having each other's backs,
But lately I see u have gotten very slack.
Can u remember that night out at the club?
U left me out to dry and played me like a scrub.
I came to your rescue when u were getting ready to fight,
I looked around and u was nowhere in sight.
Picking up the phone the very next day,
Giving me all these excuses
And telling me things are really okay.
Trying not to listen to what other people was saying about u,
That day at the park, how things came to be true.
There we were playing ball and an argument came about,
There were more of them so u singles me out.
U quickly joined their side,
And there I was left on that lonely ride.
But in my mind, I know now that u were not my friend,
Now I know your heart is paper-thin.
I really been thinking about
The situations and taking it slow,
Someday I hope to respect u again
But for now, I'm laying low.
Just trying to figure out all of them darn years,
How your mind just all of a sudden, changed gears.

MARC WORTHY

People been telling me
That u have been asking about me around the hood,
I heard u got in some trouble
With the law like only u would.
Don't call on me now, I'm not your friend,
Let me put it simple your heart is paper-thin.
Where are those guys at now whose side u took,
Did they help u become a crook?
I'm willing to bet they are nowhere around,
So, u are down and out like a silly clown.
But I hope the problem turns out to be all right,
And then u can wake up and see the light.
For now, u are living fowl and in sin,
I wish you'd grow up because your heart is paper-thin.

DEEPLY ROOTED

CROOKED COP

*Pop, Pop, Pop,
That's the sound of bullets
Coming from a crooked cop.
Every day in my hood,
There is a crooked cop
Up to no good.
Walking around looking for trouble,
Pop, Pop, Pop,
Ready to bust someone's bubble.
He really don't even care
If kids are around,
He looks at it as
Another black in the ground.
Blaming it on gang verses gang,
Down the street I hear
A sudden bang. bang.
Killing a black man
In the middle of day.
Ask him why
And he really doesn't say.
But in his report, he wrote
That the man was robbing a store.
Somehow a family saw
What went on from next door.
The crooked cop convince
The store owner to confess,
That the black man
Needed to be put to rest.*

MARC WORTHY

Scared the family up so bad,
That if they said a word,
That next, it would be their dad!
Back at the station he gets
Claps and cheers at will,
Putting a star on his chest
For another kill.
We must take matters into our own hands,
And rid these crooked cops off our land.
All of a sudden, I heard a gunshot,
Pop, Pop, Pop,
There lies the crooked cop.
For now, it is all good in the hood,
Until we see another
Crooked cop up to no good.

DEEPLY ROOTED

WALKING IN THE SAND

*As she walked but stumbled
Through the sand,
She notices that she needs a real man.
For I'm not quite there yet,
And when I come around, she will be gone
I'm willing to bet.
In my mind I'm still a little boy,
So, all I can do is play with her like a toy.
She has three kids that need
To be taking care of,
I feel like I'm in the way
Of them being loved.
For I'm a kid in heart myself,
It is now the four of us needing help.
So, I feel that I must get on my horse
And ride away,
Because if I continue to stay,
The sand gets unbearable day after day.
All I do is play games
While she pays all of the bills,
Or just lay around the house
With all this time to kill.
She tries so hard to please me,
But in her heart, she knows it could never be.
I don't want to work
And not even looking for a job,
It's as easy as taking candy from a baby,
U knows how people steal and rob.*

MARC WORTHY

I should feel guilty when her kids don't eat,
And there I am with a plate full of meat.
Or when her lights are about to be clicked,
I'm going over mom's house before
I get caught up in the mix.
She called me on a pay phone,
To tell me that the lights are back on.
But her phone is off,
And that I should come back home.
For we need to have a long talk,
So, when I get there, she ask me
If we could go on a walk.
I think she's finally fed up with me and the
Situation that brings her to tears,
This is how our life has been for about three years.
She beginning to explain how she can trip
In the sand all by herself,
And how she really didn't need any help.
She goes on to say that we need to let it be,
Until I can grow up to be a man and see,
That if the shoes were on the other feet,
That I to would be dragging through the sands,
I need to stand up and be a real man.
Walking through the sands,
Walking through the sands,
She was walking through the sands,
Wishing she had a real man.

DEEPLY ROOTED

IN THE HOOD

Just another day
Back in the hood,
Police cars are sounding,
Someone is up to no good.
Down the street kids
Are playing,
In the ally a bum
Is laying.
Crackheads are on
A constant prowl,
Out to get drugs
Someway and somehow.
Drug dealers are flashing
Gold chains
And driving big pretty cars.
U can find them either
On the basketball court
Or crashing bars.
Drunks are running
Back and forth
To the store buying forties.
Prostitutes are strutting
Their stuff
On the corner and being naughty.
Most of the women
In the hood
Are trying to find them a honey,
While others sit back

MARC WORTHY

*And wait until the government
Gives them money.
A lot of the men are in jail
Or running from the law,
On their record
They have some kind of flaw.
Keeping them down
And from getting a better job,
The system hopes they
Sit back and sob.
The children are exposed
To all sorts of crimes,
So, it's very, very hard
For them to shine.
What they see is pretty much
What they're going to do,
The question is who
Are they going to blame
The system or u.
We can change these things
Around the hood,
If we all come together
For the good.*

DEEPLY ROOTED

STREET WARS

We have a lot to learn from these street wars,
As my people battle all I see is scars and sores.
Growing up in the hood with murderers and thieves,
Doing everything they could
So that they could live and feed.
Off our people ways and mistakes,
U know in the hood people love to hate.
We all don't have anything, and some don't want anything,
But the expectation to bring,
One another straight down.
That's why we as people can't prosper,
Because we are quick to cut each other to the ground.
In this game of street wars,
As my people battle all I see is scars and sores.
Rather sells drugs to our own mother,
Having "beef" over this narcotic thing
As we kill off our brother.
Guns are getting in the hands of the wrong peers,
As bullets fly through the air,
A life is lost, and all I see is grief and tears.
Now the start of our worst fears,
For the beast begins to take over down here.
In this game of street wars,
As my people battle all I see is scars and sores.
Now as this comes into effect,
My people are really becoming wrecks.
Breaking in and stealing from our own kind,
No one is on top because we are all in this bind.

MARC WORTHY

So really all the crooks are getting is junk and trash,
Trying to sell it back to his own people for little or no cash.
It's just enough to take the craving away,
And sometimes the thief has to resort
To stealing again, on the same day.
In this game of street wars,
As my people battle all I see is scars and sores.
Even through our youth see and live in this,
I hope they learn and not add to their resume or list.
They need to slow up and look into the past,
So, they won't make the mistake of growing up too fast.
Seeing their family's torn up by different mishaps,
They should feel the need to close or narrow the gap.
Mothers looking at their daughters at an early age
Selling their precious body parts,
To see this happening hurts my heart.
Having babies at the age of fourteen,
She's not even grown up in a hood not so keen.
In this game of street wars,
As my people battle all I see is scars and sores.
Young boys are on the street corner thinking their thugs,
Only eleven and already trying to sell drugs.
Dropping out of school and becoming a scrub,
Needing to be at home under mother
Getting some attention and hugs.
Instead, they are headed straight to the jail,
Now it's really no way to bail.
Now they are crying like the little kids that they are,
Life is about to be destroyed
And feeling they have gone too far.
In this game of street wars,

DEEPLY ROOTED

As my people battle all I see is scars and sores.
All the child's life their father was never around,
Their mother had to keep running downtown.
For the father who never wanted
To take care of the matter at hand,
Ducking and dodging the child as much as he can.
This way of life is sad but it's the truth,
Our dads rather go to prison than to support their youth.
Now u see why the kids in the hood rebel,
They look up and see dad is gone or locked in a jail cell.
If the kid grow up to be a successful young man,
The father is there to quickly hold out his hand.
In this game of street wars,
As my people battle all I see is scars and sores.
Mothers don't know which way to turn,
For they are confused and the heart is in a state of yearn.
They need a way to escape,
They become a crack head by mistake.
Living only for that next hit,
That's also why their kids grow up to be misfits.
In this game of street wars,
As my people battle all I see is scars and sores.
Now it's time to skip to the next stage,
But first we must come from under this daze.
Come together as one piece,
That will take away our troubles and defeat the beast.
Our next step is to except GOD,
Through him we can overcome all odds.
In this game of street wars,
As my people begin to mend these scars and sores.

MARC WORTHY

WHEN I CONSIDER HOW MY LIFE IS SPENT

*When I consider
How my life
Has been spent.
I often start to reminisce,
About the good times,
And the bad times
That I've had.
In hope that
The one would go
And the other would last.
In a world that's
Out to get thee,
Upon my mother's wings
She shall guide me.
Through the darkness
Then turn light,
Wishing that one day
I would be all right.
Like a thief in the night
"I run and hide,"
But one day I must
Began to strive.
Toward this goal
We call success,
I have to say
I won't settle for less.*

DEEPLY ROOTED

I have come
To no conclusions,
Only a few hints,
About how my life
Has really been spent.

MARC WORTHY

CHAPTER 4
TRIALS AND TRIBULATIONS

DEEPLY ROOTED

LOCKING ME UP

Lock me up and throw away the key,
I have committed a crime.
With my pen
Grabbing and stabbing at the paper
Like it was going out of style.
Puncturing holes in my paper
Trying to finish the job.
Lock me up and throw away the key,
Because I was kicking and unleashing
A verbal assault.
Spitting expressional thoughts
Out of my head,
Making people buckle at the knees.
Lock me up and throw away the key,
Because I had them
Trembling in their socks
With my every word.
Backing them up in a corner
With nowhere to go.
They were looking at me
And anticipating my moves.
Lock me up and throw away the key,
Because I had their teeth chattering
And their eyes were bulging
Out of their heads.
The room got quiet
As though they were watching me
As my lips dripped off words.

MARC WORTHY

Lock me up and throw away the key,
Because I spoke with a vigorous voice,
U should have seen the gestures
And the unique sounds coming from them.
Because they were amazed at me
When I delivered my crashing blows.
First to the head making it spin and ache.
Next, I drove a stake through the heart
Making it quiver,
And then through the stomach
Making it knot up.
My last words cut across the throat
Ending all assumptions.
That night they should have
Locked me up and threw away the keys.

DEEPLY ROOTED

FUTURE STAR

*Let me make this clear,
This is my house and I live here.
When u come to my room,
You'll probably be run home.
With a lost upon your chest,
Don't be down,
That happen to all the rest.
For I'm a beast
When it comes to playing ball,
I have out shadowed most, if not all.
I'm a man with no respect,
I have to be that way
To keep my opponents in check.
So, don't expect
To come in my place with a win,
For your mouth will be left poked out my friend.
For I will shake, rattle, and be on a roll,
I'm just that good so I can say it bold.
I don't know why
The NBA keeps looking over me,
They are blind
For they need to
Open their eyes and see.
For I'm the real deal,
I will bring in major bills.
I'm very affordable for the labor,
U can even pay me under the table.
So, if u looking for a person*

MARC WORTHY

Who can make u a franchise,
Call on me and forget those other guys.
I'm a born to win kind of a star not to mention,
I also wanted to play in the Olympics.
My resume is dogging out bums in the park,
To beating on drug dealers for their cars.
I love to get down and dirty in the mix,
For u don't have to draft me with your first pick.
I can make dividends on my first day,
So please pick me up right away.
Don't be ashamed,
Just put me in the game.
I can score ten, fifteen, or twenty,
I have been known to score many.
So, if u are impressed, please don't stall,
Pick up the phone and give me a call.

DEEPLY ROOTED

TIME

*Time, time, time, time,
Everything happens in time.
Look at your watch
And make sure it don't stop,
Because time rocks around the clock.
U started work at around noon,
Examining the time u should be home soon.
Everything is coming at a steady pace,
Hey, u can't trace.
Time, time, time, time,
For everything happens in time.
When I looked up it was night,
For I couldn't see any light.
Time flew by pretty fast,
This day too shall past.
In time, time, time, time,
For everything happens in time.
Looked up and I was at work again,
That's right my friends.
Ready to put in another day,
U see how time ticks away.
For time, time, time, time,
Everything happens in time.
I see that I have completed another day,
So, I sat down and began to pray.
Saying, lord how I've gotten old,
U practically watch my life unfold.
In this time, time, time, time,*

MARC WORTHY

For everything happens in time.
I often wonder how much time I have left,
Then I find myself thanking u
For keeping me in good health.
I know my day will come to an end,
Yes, I have confessed all my sins.
In this time, time, time, time,
For everything happens in time.

DEEPLY ROOTED

PLEASE GO AWAY

Why don't u go away?
For u make me sick each and every day.
Why did I have to be the target?
I'm not the only person on the market.
U just picked me out to be your foe,
Beating me down from my head to my toes.
Since u came, I have had a difficult life,
I have been in and out of seeing doctors
Who cut me with a sharp knife.
They tell me that u are very, very tricky,
And that the situation is kind of sticky.
They tell me that sometimes if they cut u will go away,
Other times u can spread, or u are there to stay.
For I feel like I don't know what to do any more,
I think I have u beat and I turn around
And u are creeping in the door.
I have tried different drugs and treatments to measure,
If just for a few minutes I have a moment of pleasure.
Now I see u are back with me again,
U are trying to quickly do me in.
It came to a point where I had to go under a machine,
U took all of my hair out,
I looked in the mirror, all I could do is scream and shout.
Why did this have to happen to me?
I was always one of the nice one's u see.
I know now that u don't have a heart for good health,
I know u just want to destroy any
And everything so it's not only myself.

MARC WORTHY

The whole world is caught up in these trials and tribulation's,
It's times to turn this into rejuvenation.
Start asking questions so we can get some answers,
To this deadly disease called "cancer."

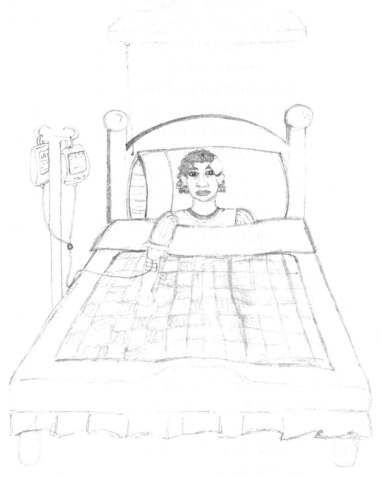

DEEPLY ROOTED

IN A SHELL

*She just lies there
As though she was in a shell,
Pondering will she go to
Heaven or hell.
Her mother speaks to her
From across the room
She knows it's too soon.
To tell if her daughter
Is going to live or die.
That's why she holds
Her head down
And begins to cry.
Her daughter can't
Hear anything,
U know what this must mean.
She's in her own world
Trying to fight her way out,
She has lost the round
But not the bout.
But the odds seem
To be stacked up,
Here comes the doctor
With some water in a cup.
He gives it to the mother
And tells her not to worry,
To put it in GOD'S hands
He'll take care of it quick,
Fast and in a hurry.*

MARC WORTHY

He walks over
To check the machine,
Making sure everything
Is okay and clean.
I pray Lord do I pray
That someday,
This girl will live and play.
Her mother began
To talk so let's listen,
She's asking the doctor
Will the machine
Keep her existing.
He looks at her
And closes the door,
He's starting to shiver
And squeak out a no.
Her mother paused
For a second, leans over
And gives her daughter
A kiss
She tells her daughter
That she will be truly missed.
She reaches over
And gives her daughter
A great big hug,
And tells the doctor
To pull the plug.

DEEPLY ROOTED

LOST

*I got a few chosen words
For u,
U better get your life right
Boo.
I see u standing there
With your head in the air,
Acting like u really
Don't care.
With those ragged
Torn up clothes,
Don't tell me u done
Put your life on hold.
If so, for what
Your piece of the cut.
Mouth all white,
Hair all over your head
Walking around,
Spaced out
Begging for bread.
I can't understand why
My black people
Go out like this
I'm saying this not to diss.
I'm hoping and praying
That u understand
That we have a place
In this here land.
The path u seek,*

MARC WORTHY

Is not the way
Your mind should be
In the word, okay.
I can recall when u
Were big and stout
Now u thin and small
Like a mouse.
U walking around
Being naughty
Strutting your stuff,
Selling your body.
Talking all skits and crazy
Having baby after baby.
I heard through the grapevine
That u really don't pay
Your kids any mind.
Leaving them in the house
To fend for self
U really need
To get some help.
Let me take u to rehab,
They really have
The gift of gab.
And when u get out,
Look a brother up
GOD bless and good luck!

DEEPLY ROOTED

MARC WORTHY

SMOKING KILLS

I really think that u have come too far,
To throw your life away.
No, smoking is not okay.
Smoking cigarettes kills,
Hundreds of thousands
Of people every year.
Let me make this plain and clear,
You need to do away with
Smoking my dear.
For each time you light it up
It hurts your heart, lungs, and brain.
The longer you smoke,
The worst the damage gets.
What a shame!
Smoking causes u to have bad breath
And stinky clothes and hair,
For it's really not fair,
For the other people
Around u who care?
To see u spend all your
Money on cigarettes,
And not to have a regret.
U just put it to your lips and puff away,
The hold pack is gone in just one day.
The nicotine becomes addictive,
And takes over your body and mind.
Now u are a goner in due time.
For u won't think about

DEEPLY ROOTED

Ever getting healed,
All u would think about
Is that tingly or good feel.
When u take that toke,
Now it makes u cough and even choke.
Smoking is no joke.
It kills more people here in America
Than AIDS,
It will have u running around for it like a maid.
It's sad that cigarette sellers are targeting kids,
Going against what the law forbids.
Selling to anyone under the age of eighteen,
Not worrying about their health
And other things.
All the sellers care about
Is making that dollar bill,
They can care less if children are killed.
So here is a good suggestion,
Put the cigarette down on the table
And make a confession.
That u have quit smoking, for u
Have learned your lesson,
And speak against this awful disease,
Now u can rest your soul
And get your blessing.

MARC WORTHY

WITH THIS ROCK I THEE WED

So now my brothers and sisters,
You're tired of smoking grass.
So now you want to smoke
The rock at last.
Well before you start fooling with me,
Let me inform you just how it'll be.
For I will seduce you,
And make you, my slave.
I've sent many of your kind,
Straight to their graves.
You'll think you could never be
Such a disgrace to yourself,
Family and friends.
You'll become addicted in the end.
You'll start by inhaling me one afternoon,
Then you'll take me in your lungs,
Very soon and once I have
Entered into your blood stream,
Running through your veins,
The craving will really drive you insane.
For it will only take one time,
And then you are all mine.
I am nothing more than cocaine,
That some people snort,
And shoot in their veins.
But when you rock me up,
I am now in my purest form,

DEEPLY ROOTED

And now a demon is born.
You'll need lots of money,
(Have you already been told?)
For I am much more to you than gold.
With this rock I thee wed.
You'll swindle your own mother,
For less than a buck.
You'll end up an animal,
Vile and corrupt.
You'll mug, rob, and steal
The craving will get bad,
You will even kill,
For a narcotic charm,
And only feel content,
When I'm deep in your lungs.
One day you'll realize,
The monster you've become.
Then you'll solemnly promise,
To leave me alone.
With this rock I thee wed.
There is no other way.
No need to look deep down inside,
For I'm here to stay
You'll know that you're hooked,
I'm a beast when cooked.
You'll desperately run to the dealer,
And then you'll welcome me back,
To your lungs once again.
And when you return as I have foretold,
You'll ultimately give your body and soul.
With this rock I thee wed until I'm dead.

MARC WORTHY

You'll give me your morals,
Your conscience,
Your heart,
And then you'll be mine.
Till death do us part!

DEEPLY ROOTED
MY HEART

Where do I began to start,
U are my everything
U are my heart.
I think about u day and night,
Even when u are long gone
And nowhere in sight.
But when u make your way around,
I'm the happiest person in town.
U have me dancing and smiling
On a high,
I feel so good that I can jump
And touch the sky.
When u get close
Like in my body
I get this "rush",
I'm hooked on u
And I can't believe
I love u so much.
I was the one that said
I would never get attached,
Somehow u changed my mind
And broke that latch.
Now that u got me on to u every day,
I can never keep u around me to stay.
Now that u have left me depressed
And with the white mouth,
I have been looking for u

MARC WORTHY

*On the regular
So, I can bring u back to the house.
I have been hunting for u relentlessly,
To the point where my muscles
And bones are in pain,
U got me craving for u,
Which I've been,
Crying and vomiting
For I'm going insane.
Trying to forget u
Like cold turkey
But I hit this stump,
When my friends bring u up again
It sends chills up my back
With flashes of goose bumps.
I have to have u back
For I think u belong in my life,
Even if it's through death
I will cut u up into small pieces
With a sharp knife.
I know I've been using u
And calling u out of your name
Such as "shag", "H", or "smack",
But frankly u mean more to me
Than a large snack.
When I get with u,
U send me on a stage of nod,
The sleeper and sleeper I get
The closer u get to my heart.
U begin to do things
That result in clogging the blood vessels*

DEEPLY ROOTED

Leading to lungs, liver, or the brain,
Now I don't want to leave the house
For I'm too ashamed.
Can u please go away again?
I'm trying to kick u to the curb
For I have been in sin.
I know that
I can't get rid of u by myself,
So, I had to turn to GOD
Who showed me to
The National Institutes of Health.
They have really worked with me
And showed me the way to go,
For u are no longer
In my system
And I crave u No more.

MARC WORTHY

SMELLING MYSELF

Growing up in a world of many things,
U watch me sprout up
To a handsome young teen.
Looking over my back because I'm so smooth,
Trying to help me dodge some
Of those tragic moves.
Well mom u raised me as best as u could,
Now I really wish that u would,
Step back and let me take over the wheel.
I'm really trying to smell myself and feel,
What's going on out there for me?
Opening my eyes in this place so I can see.
U tell me that this world is in a lot of mess,
Staring into the mirror I see hair on my chest.
Yelling out loud yea I'm becoming a man,
Now I must venture out and play in the sand.
Why are u calling me out?
And trying to bust my bubble,
Telling me to stay away from girls
And their troubles.
I can't help that I'm well-built and kind of cute,
I see that u still try to dispute.
U know I've got to have my respect in being cool,
But u are there to shatter it by telling me
To come home straight from school,
Trying to keep me from the good things
Such as drinking and drugs,

DEEPLY ROOTED

Telling me not to hang around
My friends who u call thugs.
Always asking me have I done my homework?
Testing my pride, that's the thing that hurts.
Coming behind me to see if I've cleaned up my room,
Don't u know I'm going to be out of your house soon.
I guess I will pack my bags now and just maybe,
U will treat me like a man and not a baby.
Because frankly I'm tired of u telling me
To get off the phone,
When I know I've not been on there long.
I tried to show u that I was grown
By running away,
But I was home the very next day.
I got hungry and scared of harm,
There u were as a mother with open arms.
Welcoming me back in as your little teen,
Telling me that u wasn't trying to be mean.
I say this to u like no other,
I'm glad u are my mother.

MARC WORTHY

GROWING UP FAST

What ever happened?
To those good old days?
When I was coming up
And kids just played.
We found other
Activities to do
That was all good,
Rather than selling drugs
In the hood.
Now kids are walking around
With fire guns,
Shooting at people
Thinking its' fun.
They are growing up too fast
And taking over their homes,
Talking trash to their elders
And being grown.
The young girls
Are wearing clothing
That is way too small,
Prancing and strutting
Their stuff out at the mall.
Trying to say
They are taking care of business
And becoming a lady.
A few months later
Their stomachs are out
And they are expecting

DEEPLY ROOTED

A baby.
It's sad now
Because most of them
Don't finish school,
Looking back ten years later
Thinking that it wasn't so cool.
They don't have the know how
To hold on to a steady job,
Now they are crying out
Talking about they are
Being robbed.
Turning to their boyfriends
To be taking care of,
It's all about support
It's never love.
When they leave
Or dismiss them,
They look for help
From the government
And their corrupt system.
Personally, I think
It is very degrading and fowl,
Given them these measly funds
To help take care of their child.
Their father is usually
Running from the law
Or not around,
That also causes
The child to go down.
No one is there
To lift his or her spirits up,

MARC WORTHY

So, they turn to destruction
And bad luck.
They become very violent
And start drinking,
See how our custom
Is slowly sinking.
We are losing respect
For one another,
And killing off our brothers.
We need to wise up
And take a stand,
Before our next generation
Be wiped off this land.

DEEPLY ROOTED

FEELING FREE

*I'm a bird flying so free
In the air,
People they look at me
And don't seem to care.
Calling me names
And putting me down,
Because they always see me
Walking around town.
Carrying my food
And clothes in my hands,
Living freely around
This here land.
I'm not always
The cleanest of things,
But upon my heart
It brings happiness
And I can say it with a smile,
I've been living place to place
For a long, long while.
Not really having one site
To call my own,
All this here area
Is where I roam.
Looking at different people
Suffering and shedding tears,
For me not with only
GOD to fear.*

MARC WORTHY

*Free from having to pay taxes
And very high rent,
Though my heart
Pores out underneath this tent.
Don't have the worries
On my mind about bills,
Only my honor and pride to fulfill.
A lot of my peers
Are talking about me
Escaping the plan,
I'm just beating this system
And becoming a man.
Using the beast
And his money very well,
Getting rich in spirit
Off these crooked people
That smell.
I do have some friends
That I have met in my
Many travels,
I marvel over them
And the things in them
That matters.
For I have found that their path,
Crosses my path,
For we are jovial
And rejoicing at last.
Escaping the media
And this thing we call pain,
In hope to dodge
This ongoing game.*

DEEPLY ROOTED

So next time u see me
Don't stare,
I'm just a bird flying so free
In the air.
I'm flying ya'll,
I'm flying free.
I'm flying free ya'll,
I'm flying free.

MARC WORTHY

THE OLD ME

*Peeping out of my windowpane,
It's really a doggone shame.
People seem to pass judgment on thee,
For really, it's the old me they see.
I have given my life back to Christ,
But throughout my career
I had to explain or fight.
For what I thought was right,
Now I see the Lord was always in my sight.
So, I stress leaning on him with all my might.
See all I had to do was call for him and mention,
That I will put him first and would pay attention,
To his commandments:
And listen to his instructions,
On dealing with these everyday functions.
Even though I now follow these ways,
In the back of people's minds, it stays.
What I did in the past
That seems to matter the most about thee,
For it's really the old me they see.
U see I wasn't always one of the sweetest of guys,
I used to cause trouble and tell a bunch of lies.
For my life hasn't been as clean as a pearl,
Especially having to take a lot of gambles
While being in the world.
Now being of the world as in the spirit,
My peers find it hard to believe
Or comprehend period.*

DEEPLY ROOTED

Because in their minds
They like to remember thee,
For it's the old me that that they see.
When I was out chasing a lot of women
And living in transgression,
I used to get caught up and try to deny the messing.
Calling them out of their name
And treating them like a piece of meat.
They told me I was a dog in heat.
But now I have given all that up
And have been born again,
My time as a player has come to an end.
Trying to convince people
To change their opinion about thee,
For it's not the old me that they see.

MARC WORTHY

PUT IT DOWN

Lay the guns on the ground,
U silly old clown.
Put your hands up
And fight like men,
One of us will lose
One will win.
The thing is we will live
To see another day,
And down the road
We can be friends again, okay.
There's no reason for u
To carry that gun on your hip,
What are u afraid of?
Me giving u a fat lip.
U need to learn how to fight,
So, u can stop hiding
Behind the gun alright.
That gun is the coward's way out,
Put it away so we
Can have another bout.
Instead, u rather shoot first,
That's sad.
Trying to put a brother in
A body bag.
Then the beast puts his hands
In the matter,
U might as well grab
Your escape ladder.

DEEPLY ROOTED

Because u are getting ready
To go lay it down,
That's right u silly clown.
U are going behind
The enemy bars,
U better learn how to fight
Or you're going to have
Many scars.
Your life is destroyed
There is no more fun,
U should have thought about
Putting down the gun.

MARC WORTHY

BRING BACK THE OLD SCHOOL

*My music awards go out to the old school,
Back then people enjoyed music
And thought music was cool.
I can still feel those real instruments ringing in the ears.
Those bands singing to the tune so clear.
There was no big bone women
Shaking in front of the camera so lame,
No disrespectful rapper calling her out of her name.
This is all a discredit to our black queens,
In this new generation where they allow
Their brothers to treat them harsh and mean.
We should be trying to stick together
And put our woman on a pedestal,
In this mixed-up world that is so cruel.
I think this come from lack of knowledge and understanding,
Something that our people need to start demanding.
Something that our old people really understood,
That is why their music was outstandingly good.
Not to down rap in dismay,
I like some of the rapper's music
But some I can't stand their antics and displays.
So, I must sit back and say,
Can we please bring that old school flavor back today?
Can we please bring that old school flavor back today?
I can still hear TEDDY P singing "Turn out the Lights,"
He sang many people to sleep at night.
Or STEPHANIE MILLS sending your mind on a roam,
When she sung "When I Think Of Home."*

DEEPLY ROOTED

Who can forget that group EARTH, WIND & FIRE?
Or RICK JAMES and TEENA MARIE
Singing "Fire and Desire."
These were songs so crisp and clean
BILLY OCEAN Talking about "A Caribbean Queen,"
Don't you know
I love listening to BLUE MAGIC singing "Side Show,"
Who can forget LISA LISA "Head to Toe,"
Or Candy from that group CAMEO
Those along with many others was that old funk,
We need to treasure these classics and throw away all the junk.
Just thinking back to those yester years,
When I could listen to my old school, it brought me to tears.
So, u young people better start to fear,
For that old school flavor is about to take over again down here.
For that old school flavor is about to take over again down here.

MARC WORTHY

ALL ABOUT MONEY

*It seemed to me that life is very funny,
Especially, when it comes
To having money.
People seem to look at u
In a different way,
It comes along with the amount of pay.
I can recall when I was down and out,
I could see my peers gazing and talking,
I used to wonder what it was all about.
Now I can tell it was the clothes
That I was wearing,
A lot of people used to laugh
They weren't caring.
Because they are set for the time being,
But in the future I'll be seeing.
What goes up must come down,
They don't think they have to hit
The ground.
I now have a job making a lot of cash,
I could walk around and flash.
But I'm not like those,
U know the one's that judge u
By your clothes.
They have lost much of their funds
If not all,
Who do u think they are going to call?
Yeah, that's right I'm on top again,
But I will always give back*

DEEPLY ROOTED

And try to help my friends,
For u can truly see,
That money doesn't make me.

MARC WORTHY

LET IT RAIN

Let it rain, let it rain,
The people in and around my town
Are in some pain.
We need water to pour down here,
For we are all in fear.
That someday we will wake up,
And our lakes and rivers will be dry.
That is why we're asking for rain
To fall from the sky.
Because we want to live not die,
I say this with a please and a sigh.
So, I'm talking to the Lord
Please bring water here to stay,
Bring enough so we can have enough
To sustain life every day.
I'm tired of having this
Worry on my chest,
For I know that you will
Straighten this mess.
For we need water to endure,
So, I know u have an answer or a cure.
So let it rain, let it rain,
Pour down upon us and kill our shame.
For we need to keep our
Lakes and rivers clean,
Then the Lord will bless us and bring,
More water supply,
As it come down heavy from the sky.

DEEPLY ROOTED

But first we need to come up
With a solution,
So, we can do away with water pollution.
We need to be able to
Drink good and safe water,
But throwing trash in it makes it harder.
So, I say with all do respect,
We need to keep our
Water clean and in check.
Or we might all be outside
Doing a rain dance,
So, can we please take a stance?
In dealing with this matter at hand,
Because I'm tired of this dry land.
Let it rain, let it rain,
Bring our minds back
From insane to sane.
Then we can deal with
This water crisis,
As more rain comes down we can
Then cut the prices.

MARC WORTHY

SLEEP

*I often find myself
In a toss and a twirl,
Trying to escape the trouble
That's happening in this world.
Just trying to hold on
And live day by day,
By being merry and keeping
The demons far away.
But sometimes it gets to me
And I find myself in a weep,
Crying and crying so much
That I fall to sleep.
Trying to fight off these fears
Without becoming mean,
I lay my head down and just dream.
In hope that the pain would go away,
Wishing that suffering
Would come to past,
And happiness was here to stay.
If just for that moment my mind
And body is set free,
So, I dream and dream
That peace would come to me.
Taking flight to this distant place,
Laying down the law
And then pleading my case.
My heart began to take over
In steady beeps,*

DEEPLY ROOTED

Digging into that one spot
It jars me into a deeper sleep.
The deeper and deeper I get
The closer I feel to home,
Then I find myself
At the end of the bed
With nowhere to roam.
As my snorts vibrates back
And forth against the walls,
I grasped hold
To the end of the bed
So, I won't fall.
Calling out cadence
With this long, pleasant sound,
I hope that this sleep
Will never come down.
It feels as if I'm on
This island at GOD'S station,
Ascending up to heaven
Or traveling on a worthy vacation.
I know that I have to wake up
Very, very soon,
Or my job will be calling
Looking for me at noon.
But for now I'm letting
It all ride out the door,
When I wake up
From my sleep
I will suffer no more.

MARC WORTHY

AFRICAN QUEEN

To my African queen
I must say,
That life will come
To u someday.
U will see the stars,
U will see the moon
It will come to u very soon.
By way of sunlit path
To the heart,
For u to hold your
Head up to the sky
See that your life is to
New for you
To crawl over and die.
For u are simply beautiful,
In as well as out,
Every time I see u
I want to scream and shout.
Walk proud and stand true,
For all life's tragedies
They will pass too!
For your mind is strong
And your body like a shield,
That fights off germs
And goes in for the kill.
Your smarts and wits,
Keep u battling,
And never to quit.

DEEPLY ROOTED

So, I say to u my darling boo,
Time is a virtue.
Life will fall in place for u,
U will see
And then u can come
Back and blame me.

MARC WORTHY

CHAPTER 5
FAMILY VALUES

DEEPLY ROOTED

DOWN BUT NOT OUT

*I hope that all your troubles
Are finally over,
And that u have grabbed hold
To that four-leaf clover.
So that u can come home
In a chariot driven by GOD,
I know in my heart that u
Will defeat all the odds.
I know that it's very difficult when,
U have so many people
Coming down on u,
Just remember to stay strong
In the word that is true.
Cuz, u may be lock down
But please learn
What brought this about,
Suck this up as a test
That will clear your path
When u get out.
It won't be easy at all,
But weather that storm
That will knock over that wall.
Read and get all the knowledge
That u possibly can,
Then GOD will work with u my man.
The sense of urgency
Should be on your heart,
For those angels can*

MARC WORTHY

Take u by the hands and guard
U from Satan
Who is always there?
Putting u on clear land
Because GOD cares.
I've seen your boy
He's looking healthy
And alright,
Looking forward for u
To come home and be in his life.
He's getting taller and smarter every day,
Though a lot of time
Has passed, you're in his heart
To stay.
U just need to continue
To progress by being good,
And forget those so call friends
That u had in the hood.

DEEPLY ROOTED

THANKSGIVING

People I stand before u
And cry out to u this very day,
We must first give thanks to
Our father in heaven
Who really paved the way.
The sense of urgency is on my heart,
For us as a family to put away
Our difficulties and start,
Transforming into an element
That comes into one piece,
To shed these worldly dilemmas
In turn we shall turn up the heat.
In eliminating the animosity and jealousy
That rages up between our blessings,
This family has been cursed long enough
And we should have learned our lesson.
So, can we please come down
On this day of thanks to air out
All this turmoil and negative thoughts
That may come about?
So, I can enjoy watching my
Uncles, aunts and cousins rejoice over a meal,
In hope that in the near future
We can run off the devil in becoming healed.
For no more weeping over money
Or such pitiful things,
We should invest our time in getting
To know one another that will bring,

MARC WORTHY

A better foundation for the young ones to blend,
See that chain reaction linking together like a trend.
For the old ones should be trying
To set the standard for success,
And putting away those egos and letting them rest.
So, I can look in the sky
And see my grandmother grinning down,
As her family is at peace
Spreading love enough to go around.
So, I say to u what Thanksgiving
Has meant for me,
The coming together of my family
As we build that tree.
A tree that will forever shine so bright,
There shall never be darkness
Again, and our hearts filled with light.
So can we all stand and grab each other's hand,
And then make a pack and stand
By it to the very utmost,
And let our spirits be filled with the Holy Ghost.
After all Thanksgiving is about giving thanks
To the Lord for blessing us,
What is left for our family to discuss.
So, let's dig into these wonderful dishes
That people slave over the stove,
This food is excellent for our bones
And all that to our souls.

DEEPLY ROOTED

MISSY BIRD

Thinking about u
Missy bird,
How I miss u so.
I remember the last time
I saw u,
U were happy and cheerful,
I was sad to see u go.
But I can remember
What u told me,
To always hold my head high.
I could have sworn I seen u
Up in the sky.
Smiling down at me
And telling me that things
Are going to be alright.
That night all at once
A colossal bright light,
U spoke, your voice
Echoed in the wind.
Your voice said,
We'll meet again.
Time after time
I think about u missy bird,
How it would have gone,
I know that I'm not alone.
When I say that your presence
Is in us and it grows day by day.
U can fly away missy bird,

MARC WORTHY

Not in shame
But to instill in us this
"WORTHY" NAME.
We'll meet again
In that castle up high,
With GOD leading
That carriage ride
To that big blue sky.
Thinking about u
Missy bird,
How I miss u so.

DEEPLY ROOTED

BABY GIRL

Can I talk to u?
A minute baby girl?
U are my diamond
In the ruff u are my world.
Since u came into my path,
My life has been
A pure blast.
From the first day
That I knew u were mine,
Through the
Unconditional love I found.
I was thinking only if
I'd known you since birth,
Looking back that's
The thing that hurts.
I was not always there
Through all the pain
And struggles I still care.
I really don't want
U to think that
I have left u out,
Spending time with u.
Is really starting to come about.
Seeing u grow
Into this beautiful woman,
Walking and talking
Hand in hand
Into a distant land.

MARC WORTHY

Having me there
To listen to most of your worries,
And if u call on me
I'm there in a hurry.
I can say this with
A simple smile,
I'm going to enjoy
Being in your life for a long while.
Embracing and cuddling
U in my arms,
Letting u know that
I will protect u from any harm.
I see myself being concerned
With your schoolwork and things,
In hopes that my caring
Could bring about
A positive role model,
Someone for you
To look up to and follow.
So, baby girl run on and play,
I'll be with u until my dying day.

DEEPLY ROOTED

MARC WORTHY

THE LOVE TO MOM

*Dear mom,
I just wanted to simply say,
How my love has really grown
For u day by day.
I know that I'm not the one,
Who expresses how I feel,
But I want u to know this is real.
From the day I was placed
On this earth,
I was blessed and I knew
It was not a curse.
Mom, I know it was hard,
Right from the very start.
U had to raise me and my brother,
U had to be stronger than no other.
Sometimes I could see u getting mad,
Especially when u thought
About us not having a dad.
Frustrated to the point
That u thought about
Giving me away,
Your thoughts changed
And in your arms is where I lay.
Times for us as a family
Was always trying,
I hated to see u crying.
U used to come home from work,
Then cook and clean,*

DEEPLY ROOTED

To a child u know, what that must mean.
It made us respect what we had,
And to make sure that it would last.
It builds our character to the very top,
U instilled it in us to keep on and never stop.
I also want to say thanks for letting us be free,
I really think that's the key.
Letting us experience things for ourselves
And if we needed u
All we had to do is call for help.
So, mom, I'm writing u
To say my love is deep and true.
For all the things that u do,
I truly love u.

MARC WORTHY

CHAPTER 6
ROOTS AND WAR

DEEPLY ROOTED

BLACK MAN

*Here I am a Black man
Trying to live in such
A devilish place,
Trying to adapt and overcome
An area full of disgrace.
I'm like a bowling pin
U stand me up
To be knocked back down,
But I hold myself steady
As I get in position
To stand firm on this ground.
I'm a Black man
With my head in the top
Of the clouds,
So, bring on your forces
As we battle in time,
I shall be left
With my boots dirty
And chest out proud.
For u can try to hurt me
Or have me as damaged goods,
But I'm a soldier of war
Who comes straight from the hood.
U think u slick by feeding me
That medicine that would
Affect my mind,
Or if that don't work
U try to come at me*

MARC WORTHY

Through my own kind.
For I'm a Black man
With knowledge of GOD,
Which I have learned, is power,
So, I will not let my guards down
To u even for one hour.
Bring on the drugs
And those weapons
In hope that we
Will sell them to one another.
U must remember that
They don't discriminate
Or separate by color.
U look up
And u will find yourself
In a bind,
Your own people have
Been captured in this fatal time.
Then u will try
To weasel your way out
By putting this dirty plan
On my people,
The battle we fight
In this not forever sequel.
For I'm a Black man
That understand your ways,
For I'm a Black man
That u probably try to dismay.
The word is "try"
But u won't succeed,
As my people come together

DEEPLY ROOTED

To spread this wisdom
We have hope indeed.
So, think up your next master plan,
I will quickly put a bug in it
For I'm a smart Black man.
Through your harsh
And brutal training
U taught me well.
Now I know that u are crooked
In heart and that something smells.
We must now come to this
Because I know too much,
U will try to kill me off
Like u did my ancestors,
But through them I'm touched.
Like I said I'm a Black man
Ready for this battle,
I just hope u bring on all
Your horses and your cattle.
For this will not be the easiest of wars,
But at the end of it all
My people would have finally scored.
In equality, peace, and prosperity
On this land,
Now through this Black man's mind
That's how it stands.
Now how do u want it to come down,
For it's your move, u silly clown.
Let us see how it is
With your backs against this awful wall,
U better straighten up

MARC WORTHY

Before u crumble and fall.
And take care
Of this simple matter at hand,
Because not for once
Do u see a foolish
Black man.

DEEPLY ROOTED

"WORDS"

In a place that treats us,
Like we are slaves,
They get mad when I shoot words,
At them that cuts like a razor blade.
Taking their dictionary words,
Turning them around
And using them to be heard.
They think that we all supposed
To be dummies up in the mind,
I just want them to know
That knowledge is real easy to find.
The words that I spit at them
Digs deep in the skin,
It just comes from the pain that is within.
Pouring from way down in my soul,
Choosing my words carefully
As the drama unfolds.
My words cut against the flesh
Making them bleed,
They're really in trouble now
As I begin to train my seed.
Damaging their plan from
Generation to generation,
No time to sit back and be patient.
Some of my words seem
To ring around in their heads,
Hurting their minds
And scaring them up

MARC WORTHY

To where they look dead.
Still terrified by those words that I said,
But now my heart will truly be fed.
So, I can now pick up and read a book,
Look past the disguises and crooks.
I begin to feel the energy and the notion,
Transforming my words
Into a magical potion.
My mouth is really starting to drip,
As I speak my words cut around
The stomach in one big rip.
Tearing up my enemy insides,
They know that they can't escape nor hide.
For the good will overshadow
The bad as the Lord will provide,
As my words are like music
As u can't help but hear these vibes.
As I keep spitting and my people hear this flow,
It becomes a change in time
As our mentality grows.
As we read more now for understanding,
We come from under this slavery
And start demanding,
We suddenly find ourselves in a clear landing,
Smiling and equally we be standing.

DEEPLY ROOTED

We The People

*My people, I know you hear me calling,
Why must we keep our mouth shut,
While our culture is rapidly falling.
Speaking what the heck,
Aren't we the people of color?
The chosen ones, the most blessed.
For now, I must address,
The opposition who keeps putting
Our unity to an extreme test.
I am echoing these words of,
"I Can't Breathe."
While the older warrior's die off,
An executive order is in effect
To prepare and train our seeds.
We're tired of bowing down,
But mercifully kneeling on our knees.
Calling out for this oneness,
To stop this senseless disease.
Combating these,
"Police Brutalities."
So, I say "what's next?"
My hope is to put pressure on their necks.
Or a coming togetherness I confess,
For equality we will not settle for less.
FOR THAT MATTER WE WILL NOT REST!
My brethren of color, this is a true test,
The fight is urgent oh how I stress.
Joining hands will help guide us through this mess.*

MARC WORTHY

The enemy wants us to keep bickering in between,
Rioting and making unsafe scenes.
Disrespecting of one another,
Killing off each other.
Trying to get the monkey off their back,
Hoping to keep their plan intact.
Our plan is a simple attack,
But we must first clean up our act.
No time to sit back and be patient,
We must confront this hatred.
Can we please choose wisdom,
Understanding, and of course,
To be smart.
For the love of my people
Come from the heart.
That is why we must peacefully march.
Holding our fist high in the air,
Shouting loud "Black Lives We Care."
Gathering force from everywhere.
The murdering must stop,
For we can no longer bare.
So, I say, with a stern glare,
Our Black Lives Need to Be Spared
Our Black Lives Need to Be Spared
Our Black Lives Need to Be Spared!

DEEPLY ROOTED

WISING UP

*Sitting under the tree
Eating an apple.
The more I ate,
The more my mind started to relate.
Thinking back to those early years,
When men fought one another
Losing blood and tears.
For no apparent reason at all,
Because we still have
Our back against the wall.
With the crooked and convincing
People at the head,
If we don't come together
Our race will be dead.
So, is that how it is to be said?
Put a few of us
In office for figureheads.
Nodding their domes
And being yes boys,
Then being used up like toys.
It should be called a sin,
As the beast find a way
To do them in.
It's a shame how they try
To discredit our people,
We need to wise up
To this ongoing sequel.
Start spreading the news*

MARC WORTHY

On how drugs is getting in the hood,
So, the enemy won't be
Sitting back smiling all for the good.
As we feed this to one another,
And use their guns to kill each other.
The ones who are using
Are destroyed for life or at least scarred,
While the ones who are selling
Usually end up behind bars.
Leaving our race to be the blame,
To this dirty and distasteful game.
So, I say find knowledge in self,
Flex your muscles
For we really need help.
Instill in our people
That we are somebody,
And after we smash this
We'll celebrate and have a party.
My apple is now finished,
We are to, if this problem
Don't diminish.
So just open your eyes
And see,
That we too can live
In this land free.

DEEPLY ROOTED

AMERICA, PLEASE UNDERSTAND

*America U must understand
That u have dealt blacks a bad hand.
U have brought us to this land,
Treated us less than a man.
Going back to 1955 through 1956
A black seamstress,
Was told to give up her seat.
To whom, the beast?
U can say that u are going back
To the past, but still today it last.
Sugarcoated and blinded
To the ways of life.
Not another black man
Going under the knife.
I'm seeking knowledge, understanding,
And wisdom so that I
Can dodge your prisons.
The beast thinks we are not smart enough
To learn their crooked ways.
So, we learn their education
And use it as a weapon, it pays.
Trying to put us under hypnosis,
But we are determined and focused.
To sticking to our goals,
And making the beast fold.
By coming to each other's side,
We can take the devil for a ride.
I can still hear those calls*

MARC WORTHY

Of those Jim's crow laws.
Still today we have little to say.
In things like education, business,
And poli-tricks,
It really makes me sick.
I'm trying to stress that
The devil is beating us at our best,
Turning the strong against the strong.
Giving us drugs so that we can bring
It into our homes.
Selling to one another
And rising up to each other.
How do you destroy a tribe?
Create an uprise. Get the idea,
I'm trying to make it simple and real.
Forget the streets and destroy
This so-called beast.
U need to love your brother,
Teach each other.
Principles of knowledge and caring,
It will bring on understanding and sharing.
Spread the wealth and transport
The blacks back to good health.
For we are lost in these
Trials and tribulations.
Giving the beast accusations,
Of our ways and thoughts.
We as people need to bring it to a halt.
By coming up out of the hood
And telling the beast
Their funds are no good.

DEEPLY ROOTED

When we do, pat us on our back
And don't kick us when we lack.
And when times get rough,
Smile and all that good stuff.
There are brighter days ahead,
If we stick to what's being said.
United we stand,
Divided we fall,
And that's the clue to it all.
And that's the clue to it all.

MARC WORTHY

EYES

I'm a strong-minded black person,
Who can see,
That there are eyes cast upon me.
With all my wisdom and insight,
The devil is cutting flips
And trying with all his might.
Trying to stick a thorn in my side,
I'm the one who will stride.
First to enlighten my people,
We will not stop until we are equal.
Demanding that we need
To stop being separated,
The eyes love it and I hated it.
Trying to make us a tight net,
Staying away from
Being America's pet.
We have an unbreakable bond
If we think,
But not for once should we blink.
If we do there are eyes on our chest,
There will be a lot more days of unrest.
For we are the strongest force around,
Being unified and standing on solid ground.
Knocking the monkey off our hip,
The roles should be flipped.
Now who's the nitwit?
We're going to beat the eyes down
To they quit.

DEEPLY ROOTED

*Putting their back against the wall,
Should cause the eyes to crumble and fall.*

MARC WORTHY

COMING TOGETHER

*Let the black truth be told,
We all need to look deep in our souls.
Pull out all the treacherous ways and distress,
Put it in a bag and get rid of the mess.
For we are the ones to blame,
We need to come together before
Our culture goes down the drain.
Because we are getting caught up
In the beast profession,
Coming from under his wings
Saying we've learned our lesson.
Ignorant to the point
That we fail to comprehend,
It seems to me that it's an ongoing trend.
So, scared of sacrifice
And transforming the matter,
My people would rather stay scattered.
Living in this controlled atmosphere,
I hope the end is near.
Because I personally refuse to take anymore,
Especially when opportunity knocks at the door.
It's screaming out trying to get our attention,
Telling us blacks to read 'til we are senseless.
To suck in some of the knowledge that's lacking,
In order to grab our land back.
Spread the word that u know the plan,
Getting educated is the clue my man.
No more settling for less,*

DEEPLY ROOTED

For think wise and u will be at your best.
Stick your chest out and be proud,
When u can see that day
When we come from under that cloud.

MARC WORTHY

WE SPEAK

We have been working day and night,
Forget us right.
U only think about yourselves.
Who do u think we are Santa's little elves?
Coming home tired and disgusted,
Feeling like I'm working for nothing.
We blacks are exhausted from not having,
While the beast be sitting back laughing.
Living in mansions
And driving around in fancy cars,
While we endure and our kids starve.
Always talking about
We should be glad we have a job,
What are we supposed to do?
Sit back and sob!
Thinking back to the civil war,
We blacks were supposed to score.
In peace and prosperity throughout the land,
But the beast had other plans.
Trying to feed us bit by bit.
Can we please open our eyes and see?
It's time for a major change,
Especially in this equality game.
Stop being afraid,
And let's go out and get paid.
Let us speak our minds,
And we should not be passive or kind.
Finding our place in this land,

DEEPLY ROOTED

That should be our plan.

MARC WORTHY

CONFUSED

Hey, brother man, are u confused,
Don't know which way to choose.
Color is black want to be white,
U might as well color yourself light.
Since they are feeding u
With a long silver spoon,
I hope u come around very soon.
Because right now u are being
An Uncle Tom rat,
Telling everything and being a brat.
When the enemy comes around
There u are to be found.
I see u smiling up,
They got u drinking from a poison cup.
Boy, they got u running around
Jumping up and down,
U might as well be a circus clown.
It looks like you're walking around taking notes,
Come over here and listen
To these words as I spread hope.
Trying to kick knowledge
In the form that u lack,
I hope u listen so u can turn back.
I see u pacing around looking all crazy,
Loafing and being lazy.
Finally ready to give in,
And come back home to your kin.
We're here with open arms,

DEEPLY ROOTED

We know that u didn't mean any harm.
I just need u to understand,
That we need each other man!

MARC WORTHY

RIGHT TO SPEAK

America said that we the people
Have the right to make choices,
That we can stand up and speak our mind
Or let them hear our voices.
So, when we speak against them
Is this really called wrong?
Let the media tell it
We are outcasts and our minds are gone.
I say it's a smart way to use the system,
And hopefully it will grab their attention
And make them listen.
There's also more room on the outside
Than on the inside,
So, it's better to relieve your heart
And let go of your pride.
Because if u don't it will really drive u insane,
Let it all flow out on them
And let them feel your pain.
I feel when u raise an issue
They don't want to handle,
They try to come back at u and dismantle.
Discredit u in all sense of ways,
Trying to knock u back
Or make u become dismayed.
I say if it really matters to u
Please stick to your guns and be firm,
Don't let the beast try to worm,
His way out of this particular hole,

DEEPLY ROOTED

Keep on keeping on
And maybe just maybe
U can then rest your soul.
America will probably
Act like they're interested or like they care,
But I tell u with all my heart please beware,
Make sure that u stay persistent
Or on top of the matter,
Because once u get into it,
It's going to be more meat on your platter.
They will try to lie
Or come at u in different kinds of angles,
Turn your family or friends
Against u or just mangle,
U up so that u will be that bad guy,
Don't let that stop u, reach for the sky.
And if they keep on u like
A blood sucking leech,
Just remember u have that thing
Called freedom of speech.

MARC WORTHY

WALKING A STRAIGHT PATH

I who walk the straight path,
Taunted and haunted by
The memories of my past.
Though times have changed a little I can see,
Walking on always looking over my shoulder
It feels like someone is stalking me.
In my heart I'm feeling love and hope,
Reminded of the past I began to choke,
Flabbergasted and out of control I see
That it's finally taken its toll.
What's a man to do?
Especially, in a world that's out to get you.
All my life I put up a fight,
But things never seem to come out right.
Turning everywhere looking for help,
There is none for they are all for self.
So, I say again, what's a man to do?
Just go my way too.
I thought for a second,
No, I would be neglecting my peers.
Should they too be in fear?
We are the strongest race around,
We should confront our stumping grounds.
Prove our worth in this land.
For that we must stand,
Proud and tall,
We can conquer all,
Though there are obstacles in our way,

DEEPLY ROOTED

Knocking them over could
Make for a brighter day,
Coming together holding hands,
We can make this a better land.

MARC WORTHY

LANGSTON HUGHES

*Here I am marveling over
One of the most creative
Poets around.
For all that he wrote
And had to say
He should be called
"King" and wear a crown.
During a time
When discrimination
Ran deep,
He manages to escape
In between the sheets.
To become the most
Prolific black writer of his time,
To join in on a movement
That was really starting to shine.
The movement was called
"THE HARLEM RENAISSANCE"
It helped blacks get excited
In literature, art,
Music and dance.
It also helped
African- Americans
Take a stance.
In becoming positive
Self-consciousness
And having black pride,
It was during this period*

DEEPLY ROOTED

*He wrote his best work
And took a ride.
All over the world,
He lived in Mexico,
Italy, France, and Spain.
A lot of his poetry shows
The black people's pain.
One of his famous poems
"The Negro Speaks of Rivers"
Got him fame
Right out of high school.
It was published in the "Crisis"
This gave him a lot of attention
Which he used as a stepping stool.
For his next masterpiece
Called "The Weary Blues"
This work was well received,
It was written like
A true champion indeed.
The next pieces he wrote was
Called "Fine Clothes to the Jews"
This is just to name just a few.
Even though this one
People criticized,
He went on to write
Sixteen books of poems,
Five works of nonfiction,
And nine children's books.
He was a great translator
And he wrote at least thirty plays,
For that he's a black hero*

MARC WORTHY

And a phenomenon still today.
I, a writer, have to give just due
And be amused,
By a black man
By the name of Langston Hughes.
He set the standard for us
As black writers to live by,
So, every time I write a poem,
I look up and see
A smiling face in the sky.
He is well loved
And will truly be missed,
I have to put him
On the top of my list.

DEEPLY ROOTED

M. L. KING

*I'm sitting here thinking
What a great man was he,
He gives his life
So, we could be free.
His picture still
Hangs on my wall,
Through the non-violence
Movements he stands tall.
Weathering the storms
From north, east,
West, and south,
He spoke loud and clear
His voice rocks the house.
He talked about the daily suffering,
Abuses and discrimination,
He explains how we
Could live as one nation.
He fought against having
Separate water fountains,
Restaurants, and schools,
During a time where our people
Was treated so cruel.
His name stood for what was right,
He battles with the Ku Klux Klan
Throughout his life.
Also coming together
With his congregation,
They dealt a crashing blow*

MARC WORTHY

To the bus segregation.
His expectation was to fight
For justice against impossible odds,
That's why I have to sit back
And give the nod.
To a man who is undoubtedly
One of the most
Influential people known,
Through his dignified speeches
He really set the tone.
For us as citizens to live by,
And if nothing changes
That we should keep on fighting
'Til we die.
He was better known
For his march on Washington, DC,
It really was a privilege
To hear and see.
Over 250,000 people were there
To listen to him quote
"I have a dream,"
Still today that well delivered message
Is carved in history
And reigns supreme.
He is one of the most
Appreciable thinkers
And civil rights leader of his kind,
Even though he was assassinated
At the early age of thirty-nine.
His legacy lives on in all Americans
So don't be in dismay,

DEEPLY ROOTED

That's why they gave
This awesome, awesome man his own holiday.
Dr. Matin Luthur King, Jr.,
"We Love U"
Peace and blessings.

MARC WORTHY

Another Soldier Leaves Before HIs Time (ode to Tupac)

His pain hits line after line,
Another soldier
leaves before his time.
He rapped about,
The injustice of the Black male,
The disrespect,
That we handed to our females.
He wrote,
Crippling words,
To the opposition,
Awake these demons,
So that they can listen.
Especially,
These crooked politicians.
He chanted out,
Nouns, adjectives, and verbs,
He talked down home slang,
So elegantly to be heard.
He talked about,
How our culture,
Had been raped,
And these racial,
Barriers that we face.
How,
Nothing or NO ONE,
Could take our place,

DEEPLY ROOTED

We are strong beyond measure,
If we plead our case.
At first,
He was considered a joke,
Til these devils saw him,
Uplifting his folks,
Then,
Distasteful words were spoke.
They labeled him an outcast,
Like most of the colored people,
That tried to spread hope,
Just because they couldn't cope,
With these words,
That were so heart felt and dope.
You could hear his words,
Come from jail,
How they tried to keep him locked up,
But he managed to bail.
See,
His pain hits, line after line
Another soldier,
Leaves before his time

A street thug,
They called out,
All I remember is,
A righteous brother we talked about.
They say his mother,
Was a part of the Black Panther Party,
The media say,
His life was very violent and naughty.

MARC WORTHY

A vocal person,
Who was admired by his peers,
Was hated,
Because he was feared,
He wrote,
How he shed tears.
A brother, I would love to meet,
Even though,
He got caught up,
In between the streets.
These are the words,
That he preached,
He screamed.... he screamed,
No justice NO peace!
How we as people,
Must come together,
In order to defeat
This worldly beast,
This is something,
All our elders must teach.
He was an activist,
Advocator, rapper, and poet,
Given inspiration to the youth,
And all the crooked people know it.
I'm not saying that he was always right,
But this soldier,
Went down with a fight.
So, I pump my fist in the air.
To show how well respected,
He is in the community,
And that we love and care.

DEEPLY ROOTED

His pain hits line after line
Another soldier,
Leaves before his time

A brother asked,
What was left.
Then went under the name,
Makaveli.
A man who faked his death
Quiet as it is kept.
The story is,
He still may be living and in great health.
He wrote about guns,
Drugs, young ladies having babies.
And giving praises to our mothers,
While living in the urban hood,
This man's heart,
Really was for the good.
With that being said,
God bless the dead.
Tupac,
Your name should be in the Archives,
With Malcolm, Martin, and Marcus
Who also gave their lives.
It's really a shame,
These great lives had to be lost,
For this place to change, change,
Come on yawl ......change!
We're all,
Caught up in this game.,
We need to leave the beast wounded and lame,

MARC WORTHY

And kill all this blame.
Then God,
Will uplift us out of this bind,
See, his pain hits, line after line.
Another Soldier
"Leaves Before HIs Time"

DEEPLY ROOTED

SITTING BACK

*How many of us
Americans must fall?
Why shall we always
Answer the call?
We always trying to send
Our people off to war,
This time we, as Americans
Might not score.
We are not GOD
So, we can be defeated,
Especially if this thing,
Gets heated.
Who's to say that,
We are going to win.
We have to be worried
About our allies,
Being there through
Thick and thin.
We don't know for sure
Who is really trying to do us in,
For that matter who our enemies are
And who are our friends.
But we are still there standing brave
Thinking we are gigantic,
We must remember that we too,
Can sink like the titanic.
Emotions and feeling
Are running high,*

MARC WORTHY

Everybody wants to live not die.
There is no reason to ask
The question why,
Everyone will be gone,
Just hope u end up in the sky.
We will probably be extinct,
Like the dinosaurs,
We will be missed no more.
All that will be left
Is memories and thoughts,
We need to bring this,
To a sudden halt.
We need to stop preparing,
To fight and talk,
And tell our President,
To take a walk.
He's our reason why,
We are going to fight,
We need to tell him,
To get lost by night.
For America can then,
Reach their goals,
By sitting back
And resting their souls.

DEEPLY ROOTED

WHO SCORE

*All these versions
Of war who scores,
Our people are screaming out
Saying no more.
Visions of bodies
Everywhere laying,
This is not a game of chess
No one's playing.
I hear trumpets
Making a usual sound,
There are people's heads
Beating the ground.
For u think that
The government would care,
Instead, they'd rather drop
Chemical warfare.
Pumping more and more people
Into foreign lands,
We are even over there
In the desert sands.
Tanks and armed people
Shooting rockets,
For what, trying to gather
More money into our pockets.
I say again version
Of war who scores,
Our people are screaming out
Saying no more.*

MARC WORTHY

*Families have been
Abused and used,
They're being left out
With no clues.
Especially when their families
Are torn apart,
U think that the government
Will show compassion of heart.
Sitting back turning their thumbs
And playing us likes toys,
Don't care who or what
They are destroying.
Sending more people off
To fight against their will,
Going against the word of GOD
Thou shalt not kill.
Really, they are
Creating more problems,
For there will be no one
Left to solve them.
Why do u think our allies
Are thinking twice?
They are in fear of their life.
For our foes can care less
If they live or die,
They feel like it's something
Waiting for them in the sky.
So, can I please say this again?
I hope u are listening
To me, my friend.
Versions of war who scores,*

DEEPLY ROOTED

Our people are screaming out
Saying no more.
(No more, no more,
No more, no more.)

MARC WORTHY

BEGINNING OF THE END

I heard the sound,
Of bombs bursting in the air,
People running around
In a panic or a scare.
Over the TV station,
I heard the word "WAR."
And I began to think,
What is all this for?
Is this a political scam
And if so what a shame!
Is there someone up top,
Playing a darn game?
It's not real funny when people's
Lives are at stake,
I think it's a downright mistake.
Especially when it comes,
To putting my money into it,
Not knowing the outcome,
Of a simple misfit.
Money, power, greed, and respect,
If we use nuclear,
There will be no one left,
Not even insects.
And right now,
We are at the beginning of the end,
I hope u gave your life to Christ,
And repented of your sins.
Because if this really comes about,
There are a lot of people ,

DEEPLY ROOTED

Who are going to be left out.
All that is going to be left,
Is a reflection of yesteryears,
In a world full of people mourning,
And shedding many tears.
Families being torn up,
By uncontrollable events,
People trying to run for shelter,
Underground or grabbing tents.
For there is nowhere to run or hide,
Put your trust in the Lord,
And he shall provide.
Instead of America stepping back,
And resting their souls,
They would rather be,
The police standing there bold.
Fighting fire with fire,
Or fist with fist,
Not thinking maybe if we talk,
We might resolve this.
What ever happened to
"World Peace?"
Just forget about that,
And defeat the beast.
This is what comes to be,
America's plan,
And that plan's going to take,
All us from this land.

MARC WORTHY

THE EXCELLENCY of WISDOM

Proverbs 8:10-11 (from the NIV)

10 Choose my instruction instead of silver, knowledge rather than choice gold.

11 For wisdom is more precious than rubies, and nothing you desire can compare with her.

Marc Worthy is more than a friend; he is a young man who loves the Lord. Marc is a very articulate man of integrity and knowledge, and he is dedicated to his writing with such professionalism. He is a God-fearing man and has always carried himself in a manner that makes me proud to know him. Marc is a people person and has not forgotten his roots, nor the struggle through which our people have come. He believes that if a person doesn't stand for something, he or she is subject to fall for anything. Marc primarily has a love for young people and the community.

He is an effective communicator and a born leader. Marc believes that knowledge is power. He is willing to be a role model for the young people of this world and feels that if he can enlighten just one person, he has accomplished something great. One of Marc's favorite books in the Bible is the Book of

Proverbs. Why this book? Marc knows that Proverbs is an assortment of wise sayings relating to spiritual truths and common sense. These truths give counsel that helps both to prevent and correct ungodly lifestyles. Marc knows that true wisdom cannot be gained apart from God, and that we should not rely on our own understanding, but on the truths that God teaches us, and that God will direct our paths. Mr. Worthy wishes that everyone would be successful in life, and he strongly believes what the great educator and author Booker T. Washington said: "Success is to be measured not so much by the position that one has reached in life, as by the obstacles which he has overcome while trying to succeed."

Marc, congratulations on achieving this book. You deserve it. May God continue to bless you, Marc.

REV. Anthony C. Hopkins

MARC WORTHY

Marc Worthy grew up and resides in Winston-Salem, North Carolina. His love of writing began at a very young age while taking a journalism course in high school. His first poem, entitled "When I Considered How My Life Has Spent," was well-received. From then on, his English teacher at East Forsyth in Kernersville, North Carolina, encouraged Marc to continue developing his writing skills. This support helped inspire him to become the writer he is today.

Marc has been featured in many local television events and has performed his poetry extensively. He also had a featured article in the Winston-Salem Journal and has two featured poems on the Literary Café website: "Blackman" and "Life of Sin." Marc is a people person; when you meet him, you can feel his spirit before he even speaks, and when he does, you'll be amazed. He found a voice through poetry to express himself and motivate young people.

Marc dedicates much of his time to mentoring youth through various activities at the local gym, where he spent a lot of his time as a young man. As a Christian, Marc believes that within God's word lies the answer to all of life's problems. He believes knowledge is power and strives to be a role model for the youth. Marc feels that if he can win even one soul to Christ, he has done something great. Proverbs 11:30 says, "He who wins souls is wise."

"Deeply Rooted" is Marc Worthy's first collection of poems, but many more are expected to come. He also has a CD that includes some poetry pieces not featured in his first book but will be in the next one. The CD, a collaboration of jazz and poetry, is titled "Blackman."

- It speaks to the youth.
- It speaks to the community.
- It addresses modern-day dilemmas.
- It offers solutions to these dilemmas and invites youth and the community at large to talk, think, and work together to bring about positive change.
- It speaks to spirituality and promotes a strong relationship with God as an anchor.
- It will appeal to Christians.
- It can be used in youth groups to inspire young people to pursue and discover their talents.
- It can be a source of ethnic pride, particularly for Black males.
- It's proactive and anti-violent. The poems are positive rap!

Made in the USA
Middletown, DE
26 August 2024